T0113528

Darkness

at

Dawn

Darkness at Dawn

Timothy Keyeke Mbombo

Spears Books
Denver, Colorado

Spears Books
An Imprint of Spears Media Press LLC
7830 W. Alameda Ave, Suite 103-247
Denver, CO 80226
United States of America

First Published in the United States of America in 2020 by Spears Books
www.spearsmedia.com
info@spearsmedia.com
Information on this title: www.spearsmedia.com/darkness-at-dawn
© 2020 Timothy Keyeke Mbombo
All rights reserved.

ISBN: 9781942876601 (Paperback)
ISBN: 9781942876618 (eBook)

Any references to historical events, real people, or real locales are used fictitiously. Other names, characters, places, and incidents are the product of the author's imagination, and any resemblance to actual events or locales or persons, living or dead, is entirely coincidental.

Cover Photo: Dellon Thomas
Cover design: Doh Kambem
Text design and typesetting by Spears Media Press LLC, Denver, CO

To

Elsa Keyeke

The heaviest burden that we carry are the thoughts in our head.

— Ashes to Rubies

ONE

The time was 12:15 p.m. on Saturday August 4, 2001. The place was the Diagnostic Treatment Centre, Yaoundé, a hospital not only famous for its medical testing capabilities, but also for its psychiatric patient treatment.

Though my eyes were wide open, I could see nothing since I'd begun to suffer dizzy spells. My hand groped for the chair's arm to support my torso.

"Oh, my God! Why me?" I bowed my head, sighed deeply, and descended into complete insensibility.

I had just received the worst news imaginable, news that shattered my entire being and rechanneled my life's path on earth. Life is sharply painful and not exquisitely beautiful, as some claim. Michel de Montaigne's hypothesis that human beings are surrounded by darkness with nothing particularly solid to cling to was a premise I gave much thought during my predicament.

I lived to watch my own funeral because that was the day—a dreary rainy August afternoon in 2001—I actually began to die. I, Natasha Yayuh, a virgin, had been declared HIV positive. To sprinkle pepper into the fresh wound, the test result was released by the pre-marriage counselor in front of the love of my life and fiancé, Demas. Both the paper containing the test result and the envelope from which it was pulled rested on the counselor's table as if to say, "Your hope is dashed, your fate is sealed, and your doom is clear." Other files and a couple of papers lay haphazardly in front of the grey-haired, scrawny counselor, but my blurred vision was directed only toward my death warrant which was turned to face downward. I could hear my own stomach growl as clearly as my chaotic mind, which told me to end it or tease out the root cause of my deadly infection.

At first, I thought I was dreaming when the counselor skirted around the issue in his raspy voice and announced my serology status. He had first addressed Demas's HIV status, which was negative. When he came to mine, I thought it would definitely be the same, but the way he kept talking about life and its vicissitudes scared me.

Demas, with misty eyes, cracked his knuckles while the senile counselor rambled and ranted his medical terminology.

The love between Demas and I was mutual and I knew we were doing this test for formality sake. As I slumped, the saggy, soft cushion groaned under my weight. I felt a sharp pain radiate down to my buttocks, as if I were sitting on rugged, prickly blocks of cement. My shoes, which were always slightly large, suddenly squeezed my toes as if stuffed with pebbles.

As if under the influence of heroin, I dashed out of my seat and flung the double doors to the office open, running with the speed of a hare. I could hear a voice hollering, as if from the netherworld, trailing behind me.

"Natasha! Natasha, my love. Come back! Come, please!"

The more I ran, the angrier I became. I pushed past nurses, scattering things in the almost interminable corridor of the renowned hospital. Before I realized it, I was snatched up by two hefty guards. Their firm hold did not stop me from kicking, agitating, and struggling to escape. It was Demas's intervention that made them relax their grip on me.

"Is she all right?" I heard one of the guards ask Demas.

"She's fine." Demas's voice was flat... lifeless.

"Take her to the psychiatric unit," the other guard said.

"God forbid." Demas held my hand, taking me back to the counselor's office.

Nurses, staff members, and patients streamed from all directions to ascertain what was going on. Their prying faces stared at me curiously, wondering what was happening to me.

When we reentered the counselor's office, he had his head in his hands in pensive concentration. After we took our seats, an eerie silence ensued. The last thing I remembered was Demas taking a deep breath and exhaling as if he had whooping cough. Then, the world came to a standstill, followed by complete darkness. I regained consciousness to the sound of voices singing strange, discordant, dirge-like music in my ears.

The uneasy silence was broken by a pregnant cranky lady in a tattered white gown who pushed the door to the counselor's office open without knocking. She swaggered in carrying a couple of envelopes which she heaped in one cabinet. She told the counselor that she was rushing to the Airport Road to accompany her group of panegyric dancers to welcome the president and his family from a six-month vacation in France and Switzerland. When the half-embarrassed counselor asked if she'd filled the logbook and registered all the names of those who've done their tests, she nodded at the threshold of the door. The counselor shook his head and rubbed his hands, then asked Demas to assist him in pushing the envelopes into the filing cabinet.

Though I had never sipped alcohol in my entire life, I instantly knew what it meant to be drunk. My ears and my head pounded with a violent migraine while the room spun around me. The world narrowed before my eyes and I twirled around like dried leaves tossed by a sudden blast of wind. I clenched my teeth, closed my eyes, and opened them again, hoping the counselor would tell me something different, consoling. Instead, he stroked his moustache, narrowed his eyes, and fiddled with his dark glasses on the table. His thick black lips twitched while he blinked his watery eyes uncontrollably, which betrayed his sympathy for me.

I bowed my head, feeling all my hope dwindling. I gathered momentum and attempted twice to ask the counselor if there was any possibility it was a mistake, but the words stuck in my throat. Diagnostic Treatment Centre, Yaoundé was one of the most renowned laboratories in the country and served the Central African sub-region, and it boasted new equipment and expert technicians.

My mind flashed back to the scene of the ghastly accident I was involved in a couple of months ago. It had been a blood bath and not only had I sustained bruises, I had also helped the wounded without gloves or other precautionary measures. I had no idea this catastrophe could come back to haunt me. No, not when I had come with my future husband to secretly complete the test before officially moving forward with our marriage plans.

Demas also tried to speak, but after stammering for a while, he gave up, too stunned to utter even a word. Tears pooled in his eyes as his forehead furrowed. I strained my ears to hear him muttering "the horror, the horror…" I knew it was the cry of agony of someone profoundly in love.

My eyes flooded with tears and I looked heavenward hoping God would stretch His hand and take me. I tried to reflect, but all I could see was that dark, endless tunnel. Terror flashed in my eyes. Cramps formed in the pit of my stomach. I folded my arms across my belly. It was red hot. Bolts of pain shot through my womb. I tried to move, but couldn't. My head felt fuzzy and numb and a strange sound rattled through my brain, pounding in increasing waves. It felt as though my forehead would separate from my skull and plop to the ground with a resounding thud.

I managed to raise my eyes and it was then I saw the counselor swivel his chair with his pen stuck between his teeth. His nose wrinkled as his brows snapped together. His words gushed out, but I wasn't ready for his lecture. He said something about CD4 and that I likely only had the virus, not AIDS. He also directed me to a few places where the government had subsidized anti-retroviral drugs so I could begin my lifelong therapy.

"Taking these drugs doesn't mean your HIV situation will change. It is only a palliative. Your HIV will eventually lead to AIDS. You can also be re-infected so you must take steps to protect yourself; else something worse happens to you."

I pondered. What was the point of taking medications which cannot cure you? I remembered the public show made on Nkosi Johnson, the South African lad who had AIDS but died despite taking anti-retroviral medications.

Demas fidgeted here and there. What else could be worse? I thought within me. I was already in the epicenter of hell.

As we trudged out of the hospital with my crumpled HIV result tucked in Demas's coat, I wondered what I would do. I abhorred the world and even myself. I knew that this day would rankle with me till I enter my grave to rest in peace.

Demas stood by the door when we were leaving, faced the counselor and asked, "What are the other implications if it's true that she is infected?"

The counselor waved his hands as he spoke, "Well, there is no doubt about her infection. You have seen the results yourselves. There is no one in this city or the country at large who doubts the authenticity of results from this hospital. You just have to be careful not to make any baby; that is if you will stubbornly go ahead with your marriage plans. Any baby conceived by her will not outlive its infancy…and the distress of spending sleepless nights in the hospitals only to end up losing the child."

Terror flashed in Demas's eyes and he breathed audibly fanning himself. He nudged me to move. I wanted to, but the counselor began talking and looking at me, "If ever, you madam, dream of travelling abroad, forget because there is an official ban travelling abroad on anyone carrying the HIV virus."

Before we edged out of the hospital, Demas rubbed his hands together and confessed he would still marry me and he believed in miracles. He even picked me up like a grand cavalier and swept me off into a taxicab. All I could do was rake my fingers through my hair and give a mirthless laugh.

I took him for a joker because his words left a sour taste on my tongue. I knew he was just out to allay my fears and he would later run away, perhaps to blab the information to every Tom, Dick, and Harry. No sane man could possibly walk into this trap with his eyes open.

I had lost the spirit and luster of life and was not interested in what he was saying or the comfort he was trying to give me. Paradoxically, Demas had never held me as close as he did the day I was declared a living dead. We even smooched in the taxi we boarded for home, though I did it just to please him.

True, the government subsidized anti-retroviral drugs, but the remaining out-of-pocket balance was exorbitant. How could I possibly raise that kind of money? My parents back in Ndop Town were barely eking out a living. The devaluation of the FCFA and the arbitrary salary slashes had brought my father's financial situation crashing down around them. Both my father and mother were headed for retirement within the next few months.

As we drove home, I was taciturn. My chest rose and fell with rapid breaths. I wanted to be left alone, yet I wanted to be with someone. The way the twisted test result bulged in Demas's pocket was a clear indication that we wished to shove it into the darkest recesses.

Coletta, my roommate, would have been my comfort, but she was in Dubai and was soon leaving for the UK. I envied her. She was the only one I could count on to be of any help.

When we reached Carrefour Obili, Demas suggested we go to a restaurant. I could see he was broken too, but he didn't want me to notice. He tried to initiate a conversation on lighter subjects, but it was an exercise in futility. As we stepped foot in the eating place, my nose was immediately assailed by the aroma of hot *pepper soup, bush meat, ndole and water fufu* and *eru* that wafted directly into my lungs. I quaffed a generous amount of saliva due to the congeries of smells.

The restaurant was crowded and people were mingling like termites in their colony. Some were literally standing before swallowing their food and gulping water. Others were guzzling beer while standing too. The way people were so garrulous could give one the impression that the eating house was a night club for riff-raffs. I had never been there before, but I had heard so much about the place. I had heard stories that the owner of the restaurant was using magical powers to draw customers to the eating house, which shared the same building with a bakery. I was not hungry at all. My mind was rather occupied with thoughts of my funeral.

Even in my shattered mind, I saw long tables that lay beside three walls of the restaurant forming a semi rectangle. Each table had long benches on both sides for sitting and eating. At one end of the hall was a table which occupied half of the wall. A corridor beside this table led to the kitchen and other rooms. The girls served customers on this table, where uncovered cauldrons waited invitingly.

After hunting for a seat, we managed to squeeze ourselves at one corner on one of the sitting benches. We sat at a space meant for one since the man who occupied it just left. Demas ordered ripe plantains and *ndole* for me and the same for himself. He knew it was one of my favorites and I was sure he had ordered the same plate just to please me. The sweltering heat was unbearable to the extent that I had to unbutton part of my shirt to near indecency. We only felt some relief when a group of five people left the restaurant. It appeared they had come together because they were all dressed in the same yellow T-shirts which carried the logo of a particular brand of cigarettes called Masters. When one of the service girls delayed bringing the food we had ordered, Demas went for it himself. The restaurant was pretty large, but it was not easy wading through because customers kept going and coming like goods on a conveyor belt. Immediately those five people left, another group of three came in.

Demas had to literally step on people's toes, shove others, just to make me happy. With the heat and the damp weather outside, I was sweating continually. Though all the four windows in the eating section were flung open, it still did not alleviate matters. The yellow paint used for the building was already flaking and the brown plastic carpet on the floor displayed signs of wear and tear. The noise of bones from the meat being crushed by molars, the *kring kring* sounds of spoons scooping in pots and plates, feet shuffling, and customers shouting to be served while others were grumbling that their chunks of meat were not large enough turned the place into a bedlam. Particles of food and hunks of mud lay scattered on the unkempt floor - but that was not my concern. In a moment like this, the eye is no longer interested in decorum.

"Eat your food baby," I heard Demas's stentorian voice echo as if coming from somewhere in a cavern.

"I am eating," I said, but kept staring at the food like a drunken bush baby.

"Eat, let's go, Nata," he said with a mouthful of food.

Other people directed their gaze towards me. I nodded to Demas and put some food in my mouth and started munching like a goat chewing its cud. He stood and crossed over the sitting bench before asking me what I would like to drink. Uncouth thoughts flashed through my mind. I thought of asking him to go for the strongest whisky ever, but held myself.

"Can I bring you Vimto?" Demas asked in a rueful tone.

I was lost in thought even though staring at him. He touched my shoulders softly; "Vimto Nata?"

"Yes, okay, thank you."

Beside the table where the food was placed to serve customers was a wall with an opening in a crescent shape. Customers bought assorted drinks there. It was there that Demas went for a drink. Many minutes later he came back with two bottles of Vimto and dashed back to the counter telling me that he wanted to get his change immediately since he did not trust the barman. The drinks were already opened. I uncorked one of the bottles and started caressing the sweet liquid which tasted like limestone and felt like coarse *corn chaffs* in my mouth. While Demas was still away, the person who sat next to me started behaving like an inexperienced actor conscripted to dramatize a hastily rehearsed Shakespearean play. He adjusted his sitting position, ogled at my chest, removed his wallet, pretended as if he was curbing his hands over a bundle of brand new banks notes that he appeared to be counting endlessly, and stealthily shuffled his business card towards me. That was when I really took note of him. I looked askance at him; he was well shaven and smartly dressed in a white shirt with a blue tie. He wore black pants. I behaved as if I had not noticed his antics. He touched me with the card, and I still acted as if I was concentrated on my meal.

"Wow, you look gorgeous pretty lady," he corked his head and cooed while licking his lips and flickering his tongue like a mamba. After that he leaned against the wall rubbing his chin.

I could discern that everything was sinister in his metallic voice. I recoiled, gripped the arm of the chair and remained silent.

He clutched his chest, and after staring at me furtively he said, "Please this is my business card." He shoved it towards me still without distracting the others' attention from their meal and chitchats. I shook my head in asperity.

"I am the manager of the branch of the BICEC Bank located at the Central Town that shares the same building with Hilton Hotel," he said blotting his forehead with a white handkerchief. Pretty young lady, would you mind paying me a visit to my office any of these days?"

I frowned at him. I wished he knew that I loathed his pranks with every screaming fiber of my being. He peeled off a crispy 10,000 FCFA note and was about to offer it to me when Demas came back. He smacked his forehead and withdrew his hand fast enough for Demas not to see. All along I had thought of shattering his skull with the bottle of Vimto I was nursing. When Demas sat down, my admirer ate a few spoonsful, quaffed half of his drink, lunged a chunk of meat into his mouth and concentrated on counting his oodles of money. Demas too ate a bit and left for the restroom. The man tried to talk to me but the way I looked at him made him surrender part of his meal and vamoosed, but stubbornly added "Young lady I think this might not be a good place to chat." I ate a few slices of plantain, gobbled the meat in the *ndole* and gulped down some of the sweet drink.

When Demas came back, I was supporting my head with my hands and thinking about my fate. I was already feeling groggy. I had not even begun my travails on earth. I had no time for this man who had sat by me, and wanted to begin digging his grave. Perhaps he was happily married with a family and probably had girlfriends around the city. I could imagine the spiral effect of the virus that was incubating in me, and surely multiplying at an arithmetic progression, and the consequences if I were to have any unprotected conjugal relationship with him. Demas loosened my pathetic posture slightly by gently bringing my hands down. He whispered to me to cheer up for all was not lost. He encouraged me to eat. I was forced to chuckle just to please him.

When we left the restaurant, he took me to his room, and to my amazement put a ring on my middle finger telling me that it was our engagement ring. I exhaled. He also gave me a bouquet of flowers and read a poem for me titled "Love's Fevers" he had personally penned. This drowned me in more frustration. This was a special day in my life, but it was also the worst. It was like winning a million dollars in the lottery only to learn that your mother was dead.

He had bought a television set and a DVD player. He had a

couple of Nigerian films. He put on a romantic movie and we lay in bed and stared at the screen. Half of my thoughts were elsewhere. As I imagined the two of us together, I wondered about life's little ironies and the quirky nature of fate. The news I had gotten a few hours ago was spinning my world and I could not concentrate as the idea kept burrowing into my soul. Demas was my ordained husband, but how can we enjoy marriage when I was doomed by an incurable disease which would eventually kill me after a series of chronic and debilitating ailments? My fear was not even death itself, but the mode of dying was worse than cruel. It was such a wasting disease like its bed cousins: cancer and organ failure that kept torturing their victims till their very last breath.

While in St. James High School back in Ndop in the early 90's, a campaign to sensitize youths about HIV had brought the medical doctor of the division and his entourage to our school. The pictures we were shown of AIDS patients were horrifying and chilling. I had seen walking skeletons in the place of humans, and those frightening pictures that sent shock waves down my spine had never left my memory. Since that day I had dreaded relationships outside marriage, only for misfortune to lurk at my backyard.

I thought of the stigmatization that goes with the ailment, and cursed my being. My parents would die of heartbreak if they were to learn of my situation. When I thought about them, and how they had struggled, and put their all to make them proud of me, tears started coursing down my cheeks. I tried to pretend and withhold the tears to no avail. All of a sudden, I started sobbing and sniffing. I realized too that Demas was moaning and wiping my tears. He held me tightly and prayed. It was a kind of dumb prayer, but I had no choice but to intermittently corroborate with muffled sounds of "Amen" as he supplicated:

"*Oh God Jehovah Jireh my Provider*"

"Amen," I said amidst sniffles.

"*Jehovah Rapha my Healer. You are a mighty Man in battle.*"

"Amen," I said

"You say in your word that we should thank you in all situations. Aba Father, we thank you for this situation. The God of Shadrach, Meshach, and Abednego we thank you. God of Abraham, Isaac, and Jacob we thank you. You are lord. You lifted Daniel out of the Lion's Den and removed Joseph from prison and ordained him in a palace. You are great. Right now that we are down, we thank you, and we praise your holy name… Your word says Even though I walk through the valley of the shadow of death, I shall fear no evil…Every weapon fashioned against us shall not prosper…

Honestly, I did not know when he concluded the prayer because I was once more drowned in wandering thoughts. It came a time when he was moving to and fro in his little room, and entreating God to back His Word. It was only when he held me tightly that it came to my notice that the prayer had ended. He was drenched in his own sweat. I had felt some soothing relief when he was soaked in intercession. When I opened my eyes it dawned on me that I was a living corpse soon to experience the pangs of degenerating opportunistic infections. I had to face my nightmare all through the rest of my life on earth. I did not know how I would survive the night that first day.

TWO

It was at exactly 11 p.m. when Demas opted to accompany me to my room. Unfortunately, it had begun to rain. After waiting for about a quarter of an hour to no avail hoping the rains would subside, we decided to venture out into the stormy night replete with booming thunder, fierce winds, and lightning lashing the starless sky. It was very cold that night and an uneasy silence seemed to engulf the city of Yaoundé. All the off licenses and other drinking spots were unusually closed and only a handful of cars could be spotted in the streets. Not even a single soul was hanging out that night. Demas was tucked behind me while I clung on the bike man who carried us with my teeth chattering like the beak of a weaver bird. The crumpled envelope containing my HIV test results was firmly closed in my hands. Neither Demas nor I had the courage to look at the envelope. The mere sight or even thought of it would reduce me to the depths of gloom. He had proposed that I spend the night at his place, but I was not in the mood.

Immediately after he left my dingy cubicle that night, I decided to freshen up by taking a shower in the hopes of catching some sleep. First, I creased the envelope containing my doom without looking at it. I then thrust the harbinger of disaster under my trunk box that contained photocopies and books I was not using.

When I was pushing the trunk back right under my bed I hit my wrist on one of the sills of the bed and flinched. This was the same wrist I injured during the accident that claimed my happiness on earth. Though the wound had long healed, each time something touched my wrist, I felt the pain immediately. The incident under my bed brought back fresh memories of the accident at the Yaoundé-Bafoussam highway. How I came out almost unscathed remained a miracle because the bus I boarded was a mere wreckage following the collision with truck. My head was wedged between two chairs and my arm was stuck under one of the chairs. It was in the course of pulling me out that the wound on my wrist grew bigger. Since I was one of the first to be pulled out, I immediately went ahead to assist other bleeding victims even without putting on gloves. That was my fatal mistake and I was paying for it dearly every blessed day of my life. But I had never stopped blaming the government too for allowing trucks carrying timber on such narrow roads with little traffic signs.

Shakespeare was right to have intimated that happiness like unhappiness will not last. My trouble began barely two weeks after my brilliant show at the Ahmadou Ahidjo Stadium as one of the cheerleaders on the finals of the Cup of Cameroon. By some stroke of luck, I was chosen by our mentor to lead the group and my performance outclassed all the old hands. The stadium was jammed to capacity when the ceremonies before the football match began. Our red shirts with V-shaped white strips around the chest were a sensation. Coupled with the conspicuous outfit which exposed our navels, were our mini red skirts hemmed with white strips. In addition, we wore black booty shorts that reached our thighs. We all put on low black shoes and each person held two bunches of pink pom poms.

I was mandated as leader to conclude our five minutes' performance in sixty seconds. My spirit was lifted as I sashayed and wriggled before the head of state and his entourage in stooping posture. I threw the pom poms twice with one hand and caught them with the other. I then held both pom poms on one hand and supported my waist with the other. I thrust my chest in front and flaunted it to the admiration of these powerful men. After the brief thunderous applause, I turned my back to them, genuflected and began winding my buttocks. The entire stadium went into frenzy. My spirits soared.

I faced the VIP Tribune again, and saw the president whispering something to his wife and clapping while nodding and smiling. I corked my head this way and that and danced a few steps before my time was up. I was carried shoulder high into the dressing room while the stadium was drowned in deafening cheers and thunderous applauds. The earth could not support my feet when I was finally lowered on the marble-tiled floor. Elation suffused my being. It appeared as if the whole world revolved around me. People stuck money on every available spot of my body after the football match.

Boarding the bus back to Mont Febe Hotel from where we had left for the stadium was not an easy task. It was ironclad by humans wanting to take a glimpse of me. The presidential guards and the forces of law and order were helpless before the surging crowd that kept teeming. I was surrounded by journalists who held microphones, walkie talkies, and handset to my mouth. This buoyed my spirits. My eyes gleamed as they bombarded me with questions such as: Will you like to apply for Miss Cameroon? What does it take to reach this level? Do you have some spiritual powers? Where did you train? Are you married? Money was flowing in as I was inundated with these questions.

Before our bus could finally depart, I could hear one journalist, I think from the Cameroon Radio and Television (CrTV), state clearly that "A star has been born and this lady will definitely go places."

"The sky is her limit," I heard a voice shout in the crowd.

I glowed inside. People ran behind our bus for quite some time and only surrendered when the bus driver increased his speed. I was celebrated everywhere I went. I felt like I was floating. On campus people called me nicknames like Spice Girl, Queen of Heart, and Infanta. Moving around town then was not easy as I attracted a lot of attention. Those who did not watch me live on the stadium did so on the television. My popularity increased every day and I felt as if life was made of roses. I feasted with friends. Coletta, my roommate had missed the occasion because she had travelled out of the country for greener pastures. She had complained that she did not have a godfather who would buy her way to a professional school. Demas was truly proud of me but advised me to be low key because pride comes before a fall. He also said he was too jealous, and that a lot of attention may cause someone to snatch me from him.

Those were past glories. As I thought about all these, I saw clearly the vanity of life. I saw how the once happy and proud girl had become a wet hen to be shunned by all. I found myself sniffing incessantly. I wiped the tears with my palms because my phone was ringing, and I wanted to see who was calling. I only picked up the call because it was Demas—my source of hope and the only reason to live.

Demas called me just when I was out of the shower. He wanted to find out if I was okay. I hurriedly wiped my tears, cleared my throat and told him I was all right. When I went to bed, it started raining heavily again. My mouth was dry and my tongue was stuck to the roof of my mouth as if I had been taking too many kinds of medications for long.

The storm, which continued unabated, was accompanied by blustering winds which ended up lifting a sheet of zinc from our building. Fate curved this misfortune away from me and the other tenants because it affected only an empty room whose occupant had completed his training pending graduation at the Higher Teachers Training College and had packed out about a week ago. Though the rain lasted for just about two hours, its impact was alarming. I could hear devastated students in the Bonamoussadi neighborhood wailing and weeping for the damage done to their flooded rooms.

The night was not only frightening and bitingly cold, but it was equally somber and long. I had to cover myself with both a bed sheet and my pink, thick woolen blanket before I could feel some warmth. I tried to catch a wink, but thoughts of my bony corpse kept haunting me. I cringed in my cocoon, wondering how I had erred against my God to be inflicted with this deadly incurable disease. In my mind I saw myself in my sick bed at home after the doctors had tried in vain to combat my opportunistic infections. I saw how Demas had given up on me. In my wandering thoughts I visualized how he had visited me with his beautiful wife and kids. How he stood beside my sickbed, hands folded, and kept shaking his head as if praying that I should die faster than to be wasting and wasting in pain. In my mind's eye I saw how even my parents had given me up for death. I was placed on a grass mattress in an abandoned room behind my father's house in the village in Babungo. This was the room where sacrifices were performed. This room looked haunted and scary as if it were infested with monsters, gorgons, and hobgoblins. I tried to force those thoughts from my head and bit my lower lip between my teeth.

My mind eventually came back to its normal state. I needed special courage to get through that night and the nightmare I was drowning in. I had to fight these negative thoughts before they got out of hand. At one point in the depth of the night I could no longer bear the depression. I sprang out of bed and told myself aloud that I was not going to die. I made myself a cup of tea. The water was still bubbling as I drank it, but I liked it that way. I was determined to get well no matter what it cost. I had heard of someone who was infected with the HIV virus and had decided to go into the forest to become a vegetarian. After wandering in the wilds for months, and eating only leaves, he became well. He did not know which herbs cured his malady.

Though I was seemingly and comfortably nestled in bed, my mind could not stop thinking. I thought about dumb issues. I could swear with my salvation that I was a virgin. The most intimate thing I had done was have a French kiss with Demas who claimed he'd been a born-again Christian all his life. In moments like these, nothing should be taken for granted. I must painstakingly rule out every possibility. Could it be that my test result was interchanged with Demas' since we did it together? Or maybe both were HIV positive and due to some mistake only my result was authenticated? If that were the case, it meant he was HIV positive and surely had a bleeding lip, and I got infected from his lip. I might be looking for the cause of my demise kilometers away when the enemy was within. After all, is it not said that "danger comes from where it is least expected?" I couldn't swear on Demas' behalf, though he showed signs of a truly converted Christian. When next we meet, I would look at him closely in order to see if there were any wounds on his lips.

"Shine your eyes," a voice blasted in my ears.

I resolved to scrutinize every situation. This idea reminded me of a story titled "Operation Trust None," Colletta once narrated to me. Demas might have erred just once in his life and got infected. I might have also gotten infected by the French kiss we had. Colletta was such a wonderful storyteller. The country might have benefited from her story telling skills if she did not travel abroad for greener pastures.

As narrated by Colletta: "Brenda is newly wedded to the love of her life, Gerald. She equally means everything to him and the couple is expecting their first baby soon, Junior, as revealed by the echography. While waiting for the great day to kiss their baby, both lovers continue to have unprotected sex as husbands and wives are prone to. Gerald, however, has an extramarital affair with his longtime girlfriend, Elisa, who works in the reference hospital as a therapist. She is a dazzling beauty, and according to Gerald she is faithful to him because she works at the hospital and knows the dangers of HIV and other sexually transmitted diseases. Besides, he supplies all her needs enabling her look continually succulent, nubile, and alluring. Her gentle manners and soft-spoken tone make him go "skin to skin" with her, telling himself that you enjoy what you pay for. As he argues, "you can't enjoy good wine by licking at the bottle." With that assurance, Gerald continues to tell himself that he's safe because he goes out with only two ladies who are faithful to him. His trust for them is matchless.

Elisa's world on the other hand revolves around Eric, the banker. She often has unprotected sex with him because that's the only way she could prove to him that she loves him and is prepared to marry him. She believes that with two responsible men in her life—one married and the other a responsible tycoon, no harm can come her way. She tells herself she's in the comfort zone because she dallies with just two trusted men. Though Elisa is doing everything to entice Eric to marry her, his soft spot is rather for Quinta whom he secretly refers to as "bone of my bone and flesh of my flesh." He is bent on marrying her come rain come shine. She's a young undergraduate; beautiful and cooks well which according to him were top qualities of wife material. Eric has already established connections with some politicians in the capital to buy her way to the Higher Teachers Training College as soon as she graduates. He knows that he is safe from sexual ailments because he has just two decent and trusted women in his life.

Given that Eric is fond of going out of the country for work-re-lated issues, Quinta, who is not satisfied with one man, hobnobs with two of her lecturers who not only satisfy her sexual yearnings, but repay her with marks. In fact, one of them, Dr. Edward, though many call him a lover boy, has showed some interest in marrying her. With the belief that two genuine lovers are better than one, and that it is unwise to put one's eggs in a single basket, she falls for this young lecturer and Eric. Needless to say she often has unprotected sex with this other husband-to-be in case Eric fails her. Dr. Elvis is young and flashy and Elisa's female classmates usually clamor for him with revealing clothes. His gap tooth, dimples, and twinkling eyes are so glaring which have earned him the nicknames "Woman's Dream" and "Playboy."

The other lecturer, Professor Mbifa'anyui, with whom she flirts, is a happily married man with grown up children. He also doubles as head of department and vice dean. His enviable position in the university gives her the confidence that she will pass all her courses in grand style, even the ones she won't sit in for. She has had unsafe sex with this man who is twice as old as she is.

"What intricate and ramifying story," I had interjected.

"Right. The fight for this scourge is everyone's concern," Colletta had replied.

"It takes just one person in the chain to be infected, then the pandemic spreads like harmattan dust," I'd added.

"Hmm one really needs to be careful. Without carrying out the test, I can't go out with any man. Period."

"I think the best way is abstinence until marriage,"

"And sticking to your partner after marriage," I'd said.

"But it's not easy to stay like that oh…the feelings, yearnings etc."

"I have already made up my mind. No sex until marriage. I am happy that way. No fear of diseases, unwanted babies, boyfriend/girlfriend *wahala*."

"Lucky you," she had pouted her lips and sneered.

I finally dozed off with Colletta's cautionary tale resonating with me, but with the hope that I would be more vigilant with Demas and perhaps find out from him the umpteenth time if he was actually untainted as he had made me believe.

Now that Demas had led me to Christ, I would continue to work in God's vineyard till the day I die. I took my Bible and went straight to the Book of Revelation trying to find out what it said concerning heaven. I also looked up other scriptures that talked about heaven. It was God's and Jesus' residence. This is where the dead martyrs and saints are today. Heaven is the location of the throne of God where the holy angels surrounding His throne chanting continuously Holy, Holy, Holy is the Lord our God. I could imagine the pearly streets where there is neither night nor darkness. The brightness of the city, as I envisioned, was dazzling. Emboldened by the zeal to know more about my soon-to-be-abode I took a copy of *A Place Called Heaven* by E.M. Bounds I had borrowed from Demas and started reading. I was so engrossed in it that I took three hours and a few minutes to complete. Afterwards I went to bed. Thoughts of heaven lulled me to sleep.

In my sleep I dreamt that a classmate of mine was about to drown in a crocodile-infested lake. I saved her by diving in the lake. She sustained a wound on her knee from a crocodile attack. Fortunately, I was unscathed. I carried her on my back for up to half a mile, and by the time we approached a hospital, I slipped on a banana peel and both of us came crashing down. Since I was carrying my mate, she fell directly on my spinal cord and injured it. I was taken to a specialist who treats acute and severe back problems. When the doctor sedated me and was about to administer medications, I found myself standing in front of an astoundingly dazzling gate. Its brightness blinded me. I woke up from my dream to the *tillyllylly* sound of my Motorola phone. I grabbed the phone in annoyance. Demas was the one calling to find out how I had passed the night. I told him that I was just hanging on to a gossamer thread. He told me that he would be meeting me later in the day.

By 1:30 p.m. Demas was at my door with a basket of oranges, six bottles of Malta Guinness, and some cake. I scrutinized his lips but saw no wounds or cracks. We had lunch together, and afterwards he proposed that he would tell his pastor about my medical condition so that the pastor could pray with us. I disagreed forthwith.

"Please, he is a man of God," he implored.

"It doesn't matter," I protested.

"He will only table our problem to God; that's all."

Agitated, I said, "No, I won't be comfortable."

He got up from his seat. "What if we just tell him that you are not feeling well?"

"He may want to know the exact problem."

He scratched his head. "But he's secretive as a man of God."

"It's better we just leave it," I said.

We wrangled for about thirty minutes without any headway. I wasn't going to the pastor for any prayers. Demas acted as if he had forgotten about the topic of our discussion. He asked me whether I would either like to go out that afternoon and eat some *soya*, share a bottle of drink, and just relax, or if I would like to remain indoors, watch movies and share a bottle of sweet drink. I told him I would rather be at home. He suggested I put the movie. While the movie was playing, he prepared some oranges for me. After I was done with them, he tapped his feet, shook his head and sighed, clapped his hands, and exuded a mirthless laughter.

"What is it?" I immediately asked him.

He chuckled. "Nothing."

"Nothing, Demas? That can't be. Since when have you begun talking to yourself? I've been observing your lips twitching."

"Well, I just feel that something is wrong somewhere, even though I cannot put my finger on the spot."

I winced and sank to my seat, "But the results were so clear."

"Don't you think there could have been a mistake somewhere?"

"I don't think so, Demas. I surely contracted this virus from that ghastly accident at the Bafoussam-Yaoundé Highway."

"But do you trust those rusted machines from France and those technicians who could be swayed with a stick of cigarette?"

"These are sour grapes stories, Demas. Other health facilities in this country pale by comparison to Diagnostic Hospital Center.

"Nata, bring the test results, let's look at it again. God cannot allow His own--"

"I destroyed everything."

"Nata, you will get your shock. My spirit still keeps telling me that there was a problem somewhere."

"Demas, it's irreversible. We can't recuperate evaporated water."

We agreed to attend Bible study that evening together. Demas went to his house, got prepared and came back so that we could go, but I changed my mind. I was so downcast that I would not be comfortable in church and hear others giving testimonies about God's matchless grace and mercies while I would be licking my wounds unable to testify. All attempts to convince me to change my mind were in vain. When Demas saw that I was resolute and unmovable as a mule, he gave up and left, promising to come back after the church service.

Immediately he left, I fell into my doldrums again. We never really think about our own death when we're healthy as we would other people's demise. I was so obsessed with my own death that nothing interested me. I was truly bored with life. My life was already rendered permanently hopeless at its prime. There was no point hoping against hope. It was difficult to live on the perpetual spell of self-deceit that all was well when I was literally standing on thorns. There was just no way I could feign being unruffled by its pricks. I was pestered by thoughts to commit suicide before it became known to the world that I was an AIDS patient. It would be better if I did it fast before the rumor mongers went around broadcasting to the world that I have been a deadly strumpet masquerading under the guise of a nun.

The problem now was how to get something like morphine so that I could overdose on it and face a painless death. Since that was impossible to come by, I resolved to use the Blu brand detergent. I had heard that girls have used it to commit crude abortions. I would mix enough quantity of the powder with water and drink. I knew it was going to percolate my innards. It was going to be a painful death, but it was not going to take me more than 24 hours to die and forget about the travails of harboring an incurable and opprobrious malady. Determined to kill myself, I took some coins, put on some tight-fitting jeans, a fez hat and darted out into the street. The first shop I found didn't have any detergent. The second shop did not have the Blu brand. I trekked all the way to the Chapelle Obili roundabout before I found what I wanted. The sachet I bought was more than enough to do the trick.

THREE

I was filled by mixed feelings of anxiety and fear when I got home with the detergent tucked in my hands. Given that I had not slept well the previous night, I decided to rest a while in bed before drinking the detergent. Surprisingly, I was overtaken by sleep. Again, I had a horrible dream. I dreamt that a mysterious force had plunged me into a bottomless pit. The wave of the force was so inexorable that I was going down the abyss like a stone. I was yelling for help as I endlessly floated down. I awoke with trickles of sweat coursing down my entire body. However, this nightmare did not deter me from ending my life.

I knelt beside my bed and prayed that God should have mercy on my soul. After the prayer, I read everything on the back of the sachet, ripped the paper open, and poured the contents in a cup. I warmed some water and mixed the powder in it. After stirring the paste for a while, I decided to taste a bit of it. It was really awful. I spat it out, mustered courage, scooped about half a teaspoon, pinched my nose with my fingers and swallowed the detergent. It was going down my throat with a burning sensation. The effect was immediate. Heat started radiating from my stomach to my skin. I wrapped the cup containing the remaining detergent in a plastic bag and dumped it in our pit toilet. I plodded back to my room in sudden haste.

I slumped into bed, but it seemed to be reeling round and

round like a roller coaster. My stomach started grumbling, and I developed a running stomach. It felt as if myriads of tiny needles were moving back and forth like pistons in my guts. I thrust my middle finger in my throat and regurgitated. However, this did not abate my terrifying pain. I drank a lot of water, but it seemed to worsen the situation. I took three tablespoons full of powdered milk hoping that it would neutralize the effects of the detergent. Amazingly, the pain subsided for a while.

After about thirty minutes I threw up again. Patches of blood were smeared in the mess. I was feeling seedy. The stomach pains had become gripes. My room spun and my legs wobbled as if I was standing on a hammock. Deeply distraught, I sobbed, and screamed for help, but no one showed up. I had forgotten that Papa Wemba had come to the city and everyone wanted to witness the crowd-pulling event. I did not even have the strength to get up. I flopped in bed bemoaning my fate and rolling on it from one end to another calling on God to give me another chance. I had the sensation that my innards had been entangled together in one funny heap. I was sweating all over as the excruciating pain had degenerated into a heart throbbing one. I needed to act fast. I had to fight the fiends of death since I was racing against time. If I were to go to the hospital what would I tell the doctor? The money I had from my role as a cheerleader during the Cup of Cameroon finals between Ndop Young Tikaris against Coton Sport Garoua was almost finished. I never knew death could be so painful. I thought of the thief on the cross who at the eleventh hour pleaded for God's mercy and forgiveness, and instantly received pardon and salvation, and I prayed that God would cleanse me from all my sins of commission and omission.

After the prayer I lay in bed in the posture of a corpse but remembered that my door was bolted. I crawled out of bed and left it ajar and also did the same to my window. I did not want my decomposing corpse to be discovered at an advanced stage of putrefaction. I crept back to bed and lay in the same posture with the blanket wrapped around me. I thought about my parents and my sibling and started sobbing. No one would ever know the cause of my death since autopsies were not common. Besides, who cared to know anything about a corpse? Many people would attribute my sudden demise to witchcraft, and either my rich uncle or childless aunt would be accused of having killed me for rituals. I could not imagine how Demas would feel after learning of my sudden death. Perhaps it could be good riddance to him. He might be the only one to give a clue as to the cause of my tragic exit. He would definitely attribute it to a heart attack, but he would not dare tell anyone because sharing the information would entail also giving the reason of the cardiac arrest. I was in a muddle. It was in the course of this thinking that the pains increased tenfold and my guts literally transformed into an inferno. I jumped out of bed and pleaded with God the millionth time to accord me one more chance on earth. I knelt in front of my bed and was praying and groaning when I heard a knock on my door. The knock completely flung wide open the partially opened door. I was still reeling with pain, fear, and shock.

It was dusk, and I had not turned on the lights. I hurriedly got up and wiped my tears and pretended as if I had been sleeping.

I heard the knock again. It was accompanied by Clarisse's voice, my next-door neighbor: "*Gafara, il n'est pas quelq'un ici?* No one in here? ... Nata...Nata..."

"Come in *oh*... I was resting Cla," I pretended.

"*Tu dors quoi?* Why are you sleeping now?"

"Hahaha," I pretended to laugh. "Just allow me my sister."

"I rented this latest Nigerian movie titled *When God Says Yes* and I was calling so that we can watch it."

"I am very tired."

"*Ah ah* Nata...You too...This movie will take away the tiredness from you."

"Later Cla. I thought you had gone to take your naked eyes," I indicated with my hands, "to see Papa Wemba with."

"No mi oh," she shrugged her shoulders. "The crowd that would be there."

"Ok."

"You want us to watch this movie at your place or at mine?"

Her cell phone rang. She received her call and went out. After talking over the phone for a while, she came in and told me that her boyfriend had just called that she should meet him at *Joliajo Bar*. She also said that the minister for higher education had passed out a communique stating that the date of the graduation ceremony for students of the Higher Teachers Training College would soon be announced. Her boyfriend was a graduate from that prestigious institution. She left the movie with me and told me that she had to return it the next day in the evening.

Once she left, my pains returned tenfold. I literally collapsed on my plastic carpeted floor and was twirling and twitching while groaning as if electrocuted or under a spell. I felt like I had been cursed. I thought of the hospital and its administrative bottlenecks. It would be better to go and die there, I concluded. But how was I going to go, and what would I tell the doctor? I did not even have the strength to stand, let alone walk up to the road to look for a motor bike. It was in the course of my contemplations that Demas barged in.

"What is going on with you, Nata?" he shouted after he saw me on the floor in such bad shape.

"My stomach… I am dying…"

He bent over me and lifted me up. "What happened, and your door is completely open?"

"I don't know."

"Please what did you eat dear?"

"Just normal food."

"Are you sure? Then what happened?"

"I can't tell."

"Then we must go to the hospital. Luckily, I have some money on me."

He dashed out and in the blink of an eye, he was back with a motor bike man. He lifted me onto the bike and to the hospital we went. The pain was so intense that I was half conscious. All I could hear at the university teaching hospital were demands for money and curses that I had committed crude abortion. We were told that no doctor was available to attend to us at the moment, but that if we really needed to see a toxicologist or gastroenterologist, we should offer a bribe so that arrangements could be made to that effect. I could hear, as if from a fairyland, Demas quarrelling with a couple of nurses over poor customer service and over drugs that they had insisted selling to him even when my ailment was not yet diagnosed. Miffed by the lackluster attitude of the nurses and their greed for money, Demas decided to take me to a clinic at Bonamoussadi. As we left, I could hear a nurse cursing in French "*she is angry, she is angry*" as if saying my ailment was due to anger. The other nurses were also screaming that I should be taken elsewhere.

It was around midnight that we arrived at Affordable Best Care Clinic managed by a final year student at the lone university teaching hospital of the country. After hearing of my ordeal, he gave me Metronidazole, Zantac, and Tylenol. I took the medications and lay down on the only makeshift *Volno* metal bed he had for patients. After about an hour the medication worked like magic, and I felt some relief. I was terribly hungry. I guessed, as it had often happened, almost every shop and off license around the vicinity was closed, except for "Ndop Embassy" a popular pub cum restaurant. I could hear music blaring from the hot spot's powerful loudspeakers. It was there that Demas went in search of grilled fish. While he was away, I had time to assess my environment. The clinic was just a little room of not more than five square meters. It was partitioned into two compartments: one part for consultation, and the other for treatment. Pain had prevented me from noticing these details. The area for treatment was smaller, and it looked like a cave with no exit. The little cubicle where I lay made me feel claustrophobic. This feeling was exacerbated by the very low ceiling which hung precariously as if it could fall at any time.

When Demas came back, he tasted a bit of the fish and told me that my situation had made him lose his appetite. It was only when I insisted on feeding him that he accepted to eat a little more. I savored the fish as if I had not set eyes on food for a full week. Soon the doctor, as we called him, advised that I was free to go home. He said I should return should the pains resurfaced. He handed my bill to Demas which included the cost for additional medications he had prescribed.

Demas helped me down from the one and a half-meters-high metal bed. On coming out we stood sideways and squeezed ourselves out of the cove to the compartment where the doctor does his consultations and sells drugs. He was sitting behind a table which occupied almost half of the wall. Demas and I sat on a bench capable of holding at most three people.

"Drink each of these at once," he said pointing to tablets in two little Ziploc bags.

"How many times?"

"Morning, afternoon, evening… for one week." He had just removed part of the medication from a plastic cup and added to the sachet labeled Metronidazole.

Out of curiosity, Demas decided to look at the medication container. "Doc. This medication seems to have expired about a week ago… see…" he pointed to him.

"That's okay."

"I'm not comfortable, Doc." Demas protested.

"Normally they used to give a three-month window for any drug to be completely expired."

As the doctor went to put away the cups containing the

medications in one creaking cupboard, I noticed that he also operated a mini pharmacy. I could see through the mesh of wires that shaded the old and dirty boxes of medications like Andrew Liver Salt, Phensic, Aspirin, Influenza, Ibuprofen, China balm, Omeprazole, Coughter, Maalox, Penicillin, and Tetracycline. Everything was smeared with dust. The walls of the consultation room were covered with posters advertising different types of medications.

After Demas paid him the money he requested, he bade us farewell and asked if I was pregnant.

I pouted my lips, "Why ask?"

"Trying to know if you've not taken anything to abort."

"Let's go," Demas shoved me out.

FOUR

We arrived home by 2:30 a.m. according to my wall clock. My eyes were gritty for lack of sleep. I started feeling some muscle cramps around my navel. I told Demas to examine it. My stomach was twitching. He asked me if it was still aching and I said no, but after about ten minutes, I could no longer pretend. It seemed as if I was back to square one. I was clearly weeping.

"Please, dear, tell me what actually happened," Demas said confused.

"I don't know," I replied and buried my head in my hands in shame.

He placed his hands on my shoulders. "But this is not normal."

"Please take me to my parents before I die here."

"No! Don't talk like that, darling. Nothing will happen to you."

I skipped from the bed, but before Demas could notice what I was about to do, I had already tossed a handful of the tablets I just bought into my mouth. From the look on his grimaced face I could tell that he thought I had finally gone nutty.

"Do you know the gravity of what you've just done?" he asked.

"Overdose."

"You need to immediately lick some palm oil to counteract the effect of any toxin in your system. Palm kernel oil would have been perfect."

"There is no such thing here," I slurred in pain.

Demas stomped his feet and said, "Then I must rush to my house now and bring you some palm oil."

"But your house is about a kilometer away. Besides, there are no motorbikes at this hour."

"A corpse needs not fear the coffin." So saying, he stomped out in the still and damp night.

Alone, I started feeling guilty for my dumb act of wanting to kill myself. I was so ashamed that I had to cover my face with my palms as if someone were watching me. I thought of aloe vera and decided to try some to see if it could relieve my agony. Luckily, bunches of it were growing luxuriantly in plastic buckets on our veranda. Clarisse planted them to use the jelly for her hair. I harvested two healthy leaves, scooped out the jelly which produced half a cup. Because of the bitterness, I closed my nose tightly and gulped the content. Afterwards I drank two cups of water. I lay in bed for a few minutes wondering about the cruelty and partiality of life. After the jelly had settled in my stomach, I felt some relief.

I thought of the movie Clarisse gave me and decided to look at its cover. Starring in the movie were Nollywood stars in the caliber of Richard Mofe Damijo, Stella Damasus, Clem Ohameze, Ngozi Ezeonu, Pete Edochie, and Ejike Asiegbu. I thought of trying the movie out but decided to wait for Demas. A few minutes later I heard the sound of a motorbike all the way down the road. The bike seemed to halt around the yard of the building where I lived. I was wondering who was on the bike. I hoped it was Demas. Then I overheard Demas and the bike man haggling about the price. In the end I heard Demas saying he will give him 200 FCFA. The bike man thanked him and even called him *grand frère*, meaning big brother, as a sign of respect.

"How are you feeling?" Demas asked as he bumped into my room with a plastic bag cupped in his hand.

"Which magic did you use to fly to your house and back?"

"Get up and lick it," Demas handed the bottle containing the palm oil to me.

I scrunched my face as if I had been asked to smell the droppings of a duck, feeling disdain for how I was going to lick palm oil. Since the only way to get treated was the hard way, I made up my mind to take in as much as possible. After all I had already taken Blu detergent which was horribly corrosive, and aloe vera which was terribly bitter. When I got up and started licking the oil with my hands, Demas took a few strides to where my kitchen utensils were and brought a spoon for me to use.

"Please, let me use my fingers," I protested.

"Why are you so fetishistic, Nata?"

"Tradition demands that concoctions like this should be taken with the fingers."

"That doesn't matter."

"It matters to—"

"Okay... but know that it has no influence, Nata."

"It has."

"Hope the pains are not turning you--"

"Stop it."

"Are you okay? You have suddenly become cyni--"

I sighed deeply but did not utter a word. I concentrated on licking the concoction with my fingers; grumbling all the while that it was easy to dish out advice to the affected.

"Pain can make one move naked," Demas said as he treaded towards me.

He saw the movie lying on my bed, and muttered its title "When God Says Yes" several times, and took it exclaiming, "Wow where did you get this movie from?"

When I told him that it was Clarisse's he told me that he had watched the advertisement of the movie on African Magic TV but had not been fortunate enough to watch the movie. It was already getting to 4 a.m. I thought he would be sleepy, but he was not. As for me I was as alert as a rat among cats.

"Would you like to watch the movie?" I asked.

"Hope it won't disturb you," he said.

"Go ahead and put it on."

He stifled a yawn. "I'm more than excited to watch this movie."

I lay in bed and propped up my back with two pillows, while Demas sat on the edge of the bed holding my hand. He had also come back with a bottle of Top Orange. He uncorked the soft drink, poured in cups and handed my share.

The movie promised to be very exciting, pathetic, and riveting. I could discern real conflict in just the first few minutes. Stella's parents do not want her to get married to Richard. They claim getting married to him would sabotage their political ambitions since he is a mere businessman. I told Demas that there would definitely be a problem between Stella and Richard in the near future; in that case Stella would run back to her parents for succor. That was where the real conflict would lie. It turned out as I foresaw. Richard was struck with kidney failure. All his assets could not help raise enough money to fly him to America for a kidney transplant. Stella's attempts to squeeze money from his egotistical father for her husband's treatment were in vain. The conflict was further exacerbated by the inability to find someone who would donate a kidney. Richard's brother spurned the idea of donating his. Finally, Richard's twin sister accepted and the surgery for the kidney transplant was a success.

As we watched the movie, I forgot that I was in pain. Even when the movie came to an end I felt no pain. It was already about 6:30 a.m. I wanted to make some breakfast for Demas who turned down the offer. He said he was not in the mood to eat anything. He wanted to go home and catch some sleep. I needed to sleep too. I didn't bother seeing him off as I was burned out and unkempt. When he left, I began nursing certain weird thoughts. For example, I started contemplating meeting the banker—a morbid thought I tried in vain to cast away. I also thought of trying other healing options, like consulting mediums and diviners for my predicament.

FIVE

ive days after my suicide attempt, I decided to secretly go to another clinic to redo the HIV test. My neighbors had begun complaining that I had suddenly become churlish and sullen. I had been hounded and confounded by my plight to the extent that it was taking a toll on me. I had become anorexic and was losing weight. Demas had noticed it and had advised me to be feeding myself well. He also bought some fruits for me and suggested they would increase my appetite. But I was not in the mood at all for food.

I first contacted the Doctor at Bonas who took care of me after my attempted suicide to see if he does HIV tests. He said he didn't have the required laboratory equipment. He proposed collecting my specimen to take to a different laboratory, but I refused. He directed me somewhere to do the test. When I went there, the request was turned down on the grounds that I needed my parents to sign, a guardian to accompany me or at least a would-be husband to do it with. Frustrated, I decided to go to the University Teaching Hospital for the test. When I arrived, I stumbled on people who knew me and I pretended I had come to look for an aunt who was admitted in the hospital. I left the hospital irritated. I planned to go again the next day as early as possible, maybe in that case I would not meet someone I knew.

The next day I was there as early as 7 a.m. I went straight to

the laboratory room specialized in HIV tests. The corridor where
clients usually wait to be attended to was already full. People sat
on the benches placed on both sides in the large corridor. They
looked gloomy. Most of them were not chatting, as if they were at a
funeral. More people were still arriving. Most of the people coming
for the test were in pairs. I believed they were future couples who
came to do the test before getting married. I singled out a duo who
was so conspicuous because the man looked extremely emaciated
while the woman was buxom. Nothing could convince me that the
man was not dying of AIDS. His hair had completely fallen out
and he was straining desperately to cough. Each time he coughed
it produced a wheezing sound. His vast head dangled on his ropy
neck like an upturned avocado. His Adam's apple protruded from
his tiny neck like a bended elbow. No one wanted to sit beside the
couple. Many things started going on in my mind. I could swear
that the man had surely infected the woman who was probably his
wife. He looked rumpled and wrinkled. I felt a chill when he stood
to use the restroom. His clothes were barely hanging on him. He
looked in the clothes like a young man in the body of an elephant.
He grabbed his trousers to keep them from falling off while he
waited for his wife to lead the way.

I looked away when his wife led the bag of bones past me and
my eyes fell on his lips. They were cracked, bloody, and red. It took
ages for the couple to crawl to the restroom. The stench that emanated from him could literally knock someone down. Never had I
set eyes on a bag of bones like this. I thought of my own eventual
fate. Thoughts shot through my mind like arrows since I felt I was
going to end up like him. My eyes were red and swollen, and my
feet started dangling. I blinked several times. I leaned on the wall
to support my frame from giving way. "Oh God Help me!" I yelled.
I prayed fervently that God should take me sooner than later to
spare me the anguish and pain.

My shriek attracted attention as eyes from all directions peered at me.

"Anything the matter my daughter?" A lady sitting not far from me asked.

"No...no...no," I hurriedly said.

A nurse directed me to write down my name in a consultation book. She then asked me to pay the test fee at the counter located at the entrance to the hospital. The same nurse asked me to return with my receipt once I had paid in the money. I lumbered out of the building brushing against patients, and was out, standing where hospital bills and other expenses were paid.

"How much do they pay for the test?" I asked the young lady donned in white behind the counter.

The lady crinkled her face and responded, "Which test?"

I stood aghast. She repeated herself, this time louder, but I could still not respond given that the place was crowded. In addition, dozens of eyes shot at me when she repeated the question. She became offended and asked another client if she could attend to them. I felt ashamed as all eyes pried on me. Even though I did not utter a word, she kept talking and cursing me. She added that when girls like me come to the university, we spend our time hopping from one night club to the other instead of concentrating on studies, and often ended up with venereal diseases. "When you were enjoying yourself, did you think about the consequences?" She grumbled. "Now you claim not to know the name of an STD." A few people mumbled and others made catcalls at me. "Hahaha...," she laughed mirthlessly, and stopped abruptly, clapped her hands and asked the next patient what she had come for. I bowed my head in shame as I swallowed the insults. I finally left swearing never to ever set foot on the University Teaching Hospital for an HIV test.

When I entered my room, I buried my face in my pillow and sobbed for hours and thought about my destiny. Had I travelled from Bamenda as planned, I wouldn't have entered the ill-fated bus that crashed; I wouldn't have been infected from helping the injured passengers. I had planned to travel a day earlier, but my father had requested that I postpone my trip in order for him to recover money from his debtors. When I arrived at the park on that day, I went first to my preferred bus agency, Savannah Express but due to the overcrowded atmosphere there, I settled for Amour Mezam. On account of the overcrowded agency, a friend I met at the bus agency had suggested that I should spend the night with her at her uncle's residence. I turned down the proposal for fear that I might not easily get a bus the next day. I was going to stay put at the agency until I got a bus for Yaoundé. Later, I learn that that the driver originally designated to drive our bus that morning had complained of a fever and had been replaced with someone else at the last moment. Even then, why did we meet the truck that collided with us just around a valley? I dwelled on ifs until I fell into a deep slumber.

Demas who had been frequenting my place more after the test results woke me up. Despite his busy schedule which included teaching at private schools, attending all church services, and preparing for his competitive entrance exams, he always called around to give me hope. When he was comfortably seated in my room, he peeled off one of the pineapples he had brought and urged me to eat as much as possible. He insisted that there was no medication as strong and effective as the right diet.

"Why do you contradict yourself since you had told me not to worry about the result?" I asked.

"Stress is the disease you are sick of."

"Sure?"

"Absolutely."

"Demas, the earlier we accept this and begin looking for a cure the better."

"We cannot be looking for a cure for a disease that doesn't exist."

"Ha," I laughed mirthlessly and clapped my hands. "Mr. Denial, it's a fact that I am HIV positive. I have come to accept it."

"I think we should be concerned about our marriage plans."

"Ha, you make me laugh again. We're talking about something serious and you seem to be diverting."

"I have told you time and time again that there's nothing wrong with you."

"You saw the test result. We both saw it, and we did the test together."

"I'm so convinced that there's nothing wrong with you."

"I like your faith, but faith without action is dead."

Demas's face exposed a strange grin. "Please don't go to that."

I stood up and behaved as if I was acting, but to be candid I don't know what went over me. "I am seriously considering some form of treatment, even traditional."

Demas also stood up and cried, "What? Did I hear you well? Please, please, please don't just go there."

"I think we should tr—"

"Enough. I am not interested to hear anything about any treatment." Demas moved closer to me and said.

I had never seen him this mad. "So, what do you really want us to do?" I asked.

"Have faith in God," he said reassuringly. "By the way, will you like us to take the result to any man of God for prayers?"

"No need."

"I'm so convinced, I cannot explain, but I know that God is on our side. The Holy Spirit or let me say my spirit does not lie."

"Please, I don't like the way you are spiritualizing this thing."

Upon his departure, I opted to see him off but he told me not to bother. When I asked him what the matter was, he simply said I should rest. I am sure he left my house in anger since we did not agree about any plans for a treatment.

I had been listening to advertisements over the radio about people who could treat AIDS and other sexually transmitted diseases with herbs. When I woke up the next day an idea cropped up about trying the herbal therapy. I tried to put it off but realized

that it was festering in my mind continually. Many of these herbalists were in Yaoundé, Bamenda and Douala. They had branches
all over the country.

Amongst the herbalists specialized in sexually transmitted diseases Dr. Lambi was the foremost. In fact, he had a conspicuous
signboard which directed clients to his clinic. This board advertised
the number of diseases he claimed to treat. I made up my mind to
visit Dr. Lambi. Demas was firmly against my idea of seeking treatment. I knew that since he was opposed to me taking conventional
medicines, he would definitely abhor the idea of taking concoctions
from a herbalist.

The next day I went to Dr. Lambi's Herbal Home situated at
Rond Point Express. Besides his specialty in sexually transmitted
diseases and autoimmune ailments, he also claimed to treat tumors
and barrenness. Dr. Lambi was on call to welcome me. His herbal
clinic was full of young boys and girls. That was when I knew that
it was really terrible out there. Most of the people I saw at his clinic
looked rather healthy and in great physical shape. After the custom-
ary registration I explained my situation to him during consultation.
He proposed that I should begin treatment immediately so that my
situation does not degenerate to AIDS. He said he believed that the
virus had not been in my system for more than a year. He assured
me that with his concoctions, I would be whole again. To assure
me, he boasted of treating cancer, diabetes, and multiple sclerosis.

"So, I can be completely free from the virus?" I asked in
excitement.

He licked his lips and said, "No trace of it will be left behind."

He even assured me that the treatment he would administer
could treat all other venereal diseases including cancer.

With a smile beaming on my face I asked him why the world
does not turn to him if he were all that effective and efficient. He
replied that most people dread being stigmatized. He further told
me that he had been receiving researchers from America and other

African countries, and that soon he would go international.

He said my treatment would cost 120,000 FCFA. I pleaded with him to lower his price because I could only afford 90,000 FCFA. He accepted my offer and said he would help me simply because I was a student and determined to be whole. The treatment was to be quite vigorous and that I would be treated for seven weeks. He made it clear that if I skipped just one dose, I would have to repeat the entire process.

I still had a remainder of the money awarded to me as cheer-leader during the Cup of Cameroon Finals. I immediately gave Dr. Lambi 40,000 FCFA to commence treatment as proposed. He stated that because some of the medications were perishable, I would take them in stages. Each set would last a week, he instructed. After completing each stage, I would come for the next dosage. He gave me a sachet containing a powdery mixture and five liters of a liquid concoction which looked like coffee. I was expected to consume the powdery mixture with half a liter of water. He instructed me to take it at night because it was a cleansing agent that would flush out any toxins in my system and prepare my veins and other parts of my body for the treatment. He explained that the powdery mixture was a purgative and that I shouldn't be alarmed by the frequency of my visits to the restroom. He joked further that the restroom would be my home for a while. Should I notice that the frequency of my visits to the toilet had reduced, I should take about three teaspoonful of palm oil and take a cold shower. Finally, he instructed that after this stage I should begin taking the liquid concoction, a glass in the morning and evening respectively.

I took the coffee-like medication at 8 p.m. as instructed. About an hour later I started shivering and my temperature rose. I felt nauseated and feverish. The muscles of my stomach contracted and my intestines began to seethe. Then I had an acute stomach ache which culminated into an urge to have a bowel movement. This marked the beginning of my restless bathroom visits. I feared my innards would come out. I was awake all night. It was about 4 p.m. that the urge to empty my bowels subsided and I felt truly relieved I hadn't passed out. The heartrending pain I was experiencing also reduced. I took a cold shower and licked some palm oil. I even consumed more than the quantity I was instructed to take. I then monitored my condition for two more hours once I felt confident enough, I decided it was time to drink the coffee-like concoction and it tasted sour, but I damned the unappetizing taste.

I hid the treatment from Demas even though we met almost daily. Although he was anxious to talk about marriage plans, I kept putting it off with the excuse that we should spend more time getting to know each other better. In reality, I wanted to complete my treatment before discussing any marriage plans.

After about a week, Dr. Lambi gave me another concoction. It was a powdery substance in a little box. He told me to pour the contents into a gallon of water, mix five chopped limes into it and boil until it bubbled. I should drink it warm, he instructed. I would take half a glass in the morning, half in the afternoon, and half in the evening. This made me buy a little flask in case I was going to leave my room so that I could always drink the mixture warm. After finishing the concoction, I went back to him. He gave another box of the same medication and requested that I should bring the balance of his money during my next refill.

I had difficulties coming up with Dr. Lambi's balance. My mother had taken ill and all resources were geared towards restoring her health. To this effect, my monthly allowance dropped drastically to a paltry 15,000 FCFA. I was fast becoming a burden to Demas who was barely managing to sustain himself. Even though he was recruited to teach at Matamfen Evening School at Provence, his pittance was not enough to sustain us.

SIX

When I finished the third set of concoction, I went to Dr. Lambi with 10,000 FCFA and pleaded with him to give me more medications. He accepted on condition that I would bring the remaining 40,000 FCFA in a week's time when I would return for the next stage of my treatment. On leaving Dr. Lambi's Herbal Home that day, he gave me 5,000 FCFA. That week, he called me every day saying he wanted to check on how I was doing. Two days to the completion of my concoction he asked me over the phone if I could meet him at a hotel in Oyomabang. I turned down his request after he clarified that his invitation was simply for a social meeting.

When I finally met Dr. Lambi for my next stage of treatment, he told me he would only dispense more medication on condition that I either pay the balance I owed him or sleep with him. I wondered if he was out of his mind. Here was someone treating me for a deadly sexually transmitted disease and yet he wanted to be infected by it. When he saw that I was not interested, he suggested that he would add 20,000 FCFA to the free medication he had already proposed offering me. He assured me that he would take care of my rent, food, and other expenditures.

Who says wonders shall ever end? I could not stand the man. Dr. Lambi was a huge potbellied and scraggly bearded fellow who looked like one of those prophets in Biblical stories. The size of his stomach was like an inflated truck tire. Although he was dark-skinned, his eyes and lips were red as if he was constantly taking palm wine and munching kolanuts.

My jaws tightened with anger as he continued to call me "baby, bay...bay" during our meeting. I immediately clenched my teeth and left his clinic in quick strides. Luckily for him it was very early in the morning and no patient had arrived. He stomped behind me pleading: "Baby, baby... I didn't mean to hurt you... That's not what I meant..."

"Leave me alone beast," I swung round and told him.

He held my hand tightly and looked at me with sultry eyes. I scowled at him but he wouldn't let go of me. I tried to fling my arm but the grasp was firm. He pulled out a crispy 10,000 FCFA bank note from the chest pocket of the *aso ebi* he wore and thrust it in my hands. I used the money to give him a sideways swat on his jaw. He wiped the spot where the slap landed and smiled. I told him that I would scream if he did not let go of my hand. He said he was sorry. I pulled my hand from his grip and left and as I walked away, he showered praises about my beauty: "*na temptation de tempt me baby... you too fine plenty.*"

When I got home, I saw a note slipped under my door by Demas. I had left my phone which was turned off on the charger. His note stated that his father had just called him that morning requesting him to report to the village as soon as possible. The note indicated that he was at the Amour Mezam Bus agency. As soon as I finished reading the note I forgot about my phone and raced to the road. I took a bike and within a few minutes I was at the bus agency. Unfortunately, I arrived when the bus was backing off to leave. By the time I could find Demas on the seventy-seat bus, it was already leaving. His eyes met mine. He was struggling to say something but with the thundering engine of the bus and loudspeakers blaring in the drinking spots around, and what else I don't know that early morning, I missed it. He struggled and indicated with his hand that he would call me. We waved to each other as the bus glided away.

I decided to walk back home though I was tired and anxious. I convinced myself that a long walk back home would release some of the day's stress. Just watching people move up and down, the engines of cars, and a medley of music was invigorating. All along, I wondered why Demas's father had called him to report home immediately. There was no doubt that his father was a no-nonsense man, but I could not figure out the reason for his sudden action. Was someone in the family seriously sick or he himself? But at least he would have given a hint to his son about what was afoot. This man commanded considerable influence in his son's life as he'd told me. And Demas respected and feared him.

I met Clarisse at home taking her clothes to the laundromat. Her boyfriend, Valentine, was graduating on Friday and Clarisse told me that he had organized what she called *grande party* to celebrate. She invited me to attend the party.

"Hope you don't fail me this time around," Clarisse said.

I just gave her a wry smile.

"I don't like the way you behave. You hardly go out," she said.

"I do go out. Just that night clubs, partying, and things like that aren't my forte."

"But, Nata, make this one a date. Being a recluse will only drown you into frustration."

"I will see."

"Stop saying that," Clarise said. "Your place is reserved. It will be *mmwwaamm*…" she smacked her lips as she hit her mouth with her right palm.

"Where is it again?"

"Grand Canary… 10 p.m. till dawn."

Since I was bored and lonely, I decided to attend the party; maybe that would drown my woes. I wished I could attend it with Demas. I had tried calling him a couple of times, but the network was poor. I was worried and anxious to hear from him. I reluctantly arrived the party venue at 11 p.m. when it was just about to begin. The surrounding area was crowded. At the gate to the hotel someone greeted me with familiarity, but I didn't recognize him.

"Young lady you seem not to know me," he drew closer, adjusted his goggles and whispered.

"Right."

"Young lady, I met you sometime in a restaurant at Obili."

"Oh yes, yes, yes…," I shook my head pretending not to remember him.

"So how are you?"

"I'm okay."

"Glad to meet you after a while."

"I still don't get it."

"Remember I told you to meet me at BICEC Bank, Hilton Hotel."

He dipped his hands in his pocket as if searching for something to give me, then his phone rang. He asked for permission and moved away to answer his call. Although he seemed engulfed on the phone, he didn't take his eyes off me. More people thronged the area and blocked him from seeing me. I seized the chance, mingled in the crowd and disappeared into the hall.

When I squeezed myself into the dimly lit hall I marveled at the decor. Assorted multicolored lights twinkled on the ceiling like stars. Two ceiling fans in motion added to the beauty of the bulbs. The tables, chairs, and windows were decorated in blue and white. Each table had a bouquet of flowers in ornamental flower vases. Assorted bottles of wine, glasses and a few china lay temptingly on the tables. The stage was decorated with red, green, and white material. Two giant speakers by the stage planted on long poles convinced me that it was a "grand occasion" as Clarisse had said. I could see the DJ with large earphones on his ears manipulating his gear. Oriental Brothers' International Band was playing "Kelechi" on the loudspeakers. Most of the seats were occupied. Some people were standing. Light refreshment was already being served. Everything was gay and I realized that most people were swaying to the rhythm of the old-timer's music. Some were merely nodding their heads or tapping their feet on the blue and white carpeted floor. I stood at one corner, my eyes roving around hunting for a comfortable and hidden place.

It seemed Clarisse spotted me struggling for a seat because she came and ushered me to join three other individuals. A lady was sandwiched in the middle of two men. They were all drinking and chatting excitedly. Immediately I sat down one of the men shouted, "Equation balance. That's why I respect you Cla," he then tapped her back.

"Dare not bother my sister because she's a Christian," she said and disappeared telling me to make myself comfortable.

When Clarice left, I shook hands with the new acquaintances. They motioned to me to eat and drink. One of the men gave me a cup and I poured myself some Fanta.

"Eh…eh…what's that?" shouted the man who had said "equation balance".

I was at a loss and asked him what was amiss. He said I shouldn't be drinking too much sweet stuff, which he called diabetes, and instead drink Guinness which he shouted, "is good for you."

"Haven't you heard she is Christian?" Snapped the other man who had been calm all along.

Before the other could reply, one smartly dressed man swaggered to our table and shook our hands. He took the cup of the lady who sat in-between the two men and guzzled its content. He refilled the cup and quaffed the beer in it. After that, he filled the glass halfway and offered to the lady whose cup it was.

He turned to me and said, "Woman you look so luscious."

That was when I really saw how sparkling clean he was. He wore a blue jeans jacket over a white t-shirt. His blue jean pants and white Reebok brand tennis was a perfect match.

"I am talking to you," he looked at me and said.

"Leave her alone," the other lady said.

He turned to the other loquacious man and asked him to buy him cigarettes. "I don't give cigarettes to people" he responded.

"Is it that you don't have money, or you don't just want to buy?

"I don't have money," he snorted.

"Ha," he laughed provocatively and said, "money is like HIV, when you ask, everyone says they don't have it."

This comment, though ignorantly made, shot through my heart like a poisonous thorn. I felt uncomfortable and bowed my head in shame. When I lifted my head again, I saw him disappearing into the crowd.

A smartly dressed young man in a groovy three-piece suit came forward jauntily and took the microphone. His appearance reminded me of Demas. The emcee was brief in his salutation stating that it was not a speech-making event, but an occasion to drink, eat, and be merry. He was ebullient and used jokes and analogies that made the place exciting and funky, because each time he spoke, people would respond in thunderous clapping and the DJ would manipulate his instruments to sound like jazz.

The emcee said that the population that had jammed the large hall had disproved The Book of Wisdom by attesting that a prophet could be known in his hometown. Many people laughed, cheered, and clapped when he said this. He introduced Valentine as a remarkable young teacher with tremendous talent. When he sat down Clarisse went and whispered something in his ear and handed a piece of paper to him. He looked at the note and smiled as she tried to point to him the direction where I was sitting.

The gaiety brought sad memories to me. I would not live long enough to experience a graduation from a professional institution. If Demas gained admission into the Higher School of Mass Communication, I would steal the show during his graduation ceremony.

But the question that remained unanswered was would he still be in love with me?

When Clarisse's boyfriend was handed the microphone, he thanked everyone who made it to the occasion. He cited some of the trials he went through while in school but thanked everyone who helped him spiritually, morally, and physically to sail through the "raging tides." He encouraged everyone to eat and drink to their satisfaction for as he put it "time for battle is over…only feasting, feasting…" He joked that he would be at the door to the hall as chief whip and would only fling the doors open at 6 a.m. Before he sat down, he mimicked the emcee by quipping that the mammoth populace had disobeyed the Bible by making a prophet known in his hometown. His brief speech was followed by light refreshment. After almost everyone had eaten and the guests were nursing their drinks, the DJ stole the show. He paired people to open the floor. Surprisingly, the emcee asked me to open the floor with Clarisse's boyfriend's uncle. I remained rooted to the floor when I heard this. I was still dazed when Clarisse nudged me.

The man, who was a real kook, strode towards me with all alacrity in strict military style. Throwing all caution to the wind, he held me from the waist and led me to the dancing arena. I must confess that only my body moved towards that spot, for my spirit was not in it at all. People clapped, jeered, booed, and made catcalls as we glided to the open space. The white-tiled floor glided as if okra had been smeared on it. I don't know how I got there. But I remember I marched beside him as if I was under a spell. All other dancers naturally got up and met their partners. The music the DJ chose was "I Need Some Love" by Grace Decca. I had never been a dancer, much less opened the floor before gazing eyes. As the music boomed this man flouted all etiquette and held me closer to himself, rubbing my hips as if I were his wife. There was absolutely nothing I could do. Any awkward move by me would have only shown how antisocial I was. I just stood in his arms, a sea of eyes peering at me, praying for the two minutes which seemed like hours to glide on swiftly. I was relieved when the song ended. The DJ suggested that people could continue with their partners as he put on another song. This was the latest *zouk*. My dance partner tried to seize my hand but I slithered away, and almost stumbled in my high heels.

After playing *zouk* for a couple of minutes the DJ switched to makossa and people became more excited to dance. He put different songs changing them at random. People were dancing and taking quick brakes to wine and dine since there was excess food and drink. Many people requested to dance with me, but I refused. I preferred watching others having fun since Demas wasn't around for us to dance out some of the stress. Ever since he went to the village, he'd not called me. I had even attempted calling him twice while at the party, but my call went to the voicemail. I supposed it was due to connection problems. My appetite was sharpened at the party. I had not eaten the way I did that night since the day I got my test results. I ravished *water fufu* and *eru, achu*, and *puff puff*. I even reserved some food to take home. The party dragged on right to the wee hours of the morning. Before it ended many young men attempted taking my phone number which I refused to give.

It was difficult getting a means of transportation home that cold morning. Coincidentally, the BICEC manager, whom I had not met again since we spoke at the gate, came to my aid and offered to give me a lift. I had been waiting by the roadside for too long and was shivering. At first, I hesitated but thought otherwise. Matters were complicated because Clarisse had planned to go to her boyfriend's apartment. She encouraged me to accept the lift rather than risk my life walking home. The banker tried to engage me in a conversation but I was too exhausted to talk. As we drove along, he sought to have my phone number, remarking that the world throve on connections. He said, "Man without man is no humanity." I gave him my number reluctantly.

When he dropped me off, he insisted on giving me some money, but I refused. He forced the money into my handbag telling me that it was just a token for me to buy airtime so that he could call me. When he drove off, I decided to find out what he had put in my bag. Lo and behold it was a brand new crispy 10,000 FCFA note. My hands trembled and my heart thumbed as I held the bank note. I thought of folding and dumping it in the nearby bushes but realized that it would have no impact since he'd left.

I entered my room at 5:20 a.m. and before I crawled to bed, I turned on my phone on after charging it and realized that I had a message. My eyes were gritty for want of sleep. I managed to look at it. It read: *Hi Natasha. I am Captain Johnson who opened the floor with you. I like the way we danced. I got your number from Clarisse. Was just checking if you got home safely. Will give you a call later in the day... Chao!*

SEVEN

If not for Valentine's cousin's call that rattled my quiet sleep I would have continued dozing for hours. Since I suspected he was the one, I stopped the call. It was already about 11 a.m., so I lay back in bed. He rang my phone again. I picked up the call. When I said hello in a harsh tone, he hesitated. I said gruffly, "Who's on the line?" before he responded.

"Good morning… eh…eh… was trying to see if you arrived safely," he faltered.

"I did. Thanks."

"So how did you enjoy the party?"

"Can't say."

"How is your program for the day?"

I was silent. He rephrased the question. "I wonder if you will be out today."

"Why ask?"

"I thought we could share a bottle of Fanta."

"I'm not interested," I said and hung up.

My program that day was to go to Demas's house to check if he was back. When I went there, he was not yet back from the village. It was from Demas's neighbor that I got scraps of information as to why he left so abruptly. She was blunt. She said Demas was home for his marriage arrangements. I thought she did not know the Demas I came to ask after. My world was turning upside down.

I just could not believe the message the neighbor relayed to me. Maybe she was jealous and wanted to plunge me deeper into the abyss of despair so that she could turn around and snatch Demas who was definitely every woman's dream.

Demas could not confide in someone other than me. I left Demas's house with my head still high in the air. But my only worry was that he had not communicated with me since he traveled. He had been out for three days and we had not yet exchanged mere greetings. I had tried calling him several times but his phone was not going through. I decided to pay a visit to my classmate Emelda. On my way, my phone indicated that I had a text message. It was the banker finding out if I had received the airtime he sent. That was when I checked my phone and realized I had been sent 2,000 FCFA worth of airtime credit. I called him and thanked him for the gesture. I reached Emelda's house just when she was about to head out to do her hair. I accompanied her to the salon.

When I came back to my room at 7 p.m., I was shocked to meet the Bank manager's car parked by the side of the road around my house. At first, I thought it was an April fool's joke. It was only at a closer look that things became as clear as the stars. Comfortably seated in the front seat was the bank manager himself. I pretended as if I had not seen him or his car and was heading towards my room when he called out to me appealingly. I still pretended as if I had not heard. He wound down the window of his car completely and called louder. I regretted why I told him my name. Each time he'd asked for it while in his Mercedes, I'd waved it aside. He had pestered me until there was nothing I could do. So, when he called again louder, I swung round on the other side and faced him.

"Natasha, it's me, Jonathan, the manager of BICEC Bank," he said entreatingly.

"Good evening sir, hope you're not policing me."

He smiled in the dim light in his car, "No, no, no... I am coming from a friend's house."

"Then what are you doing here?" I asked.

"I saw you from afar and decided to stop to say hi."

"Thanks."

"Would you mind sharing a bottle of sweet drink with me? I know you students don't drink beer."

"We don't, thanks," I responded and was about turning to head to my room when he came out of his car and walked across the road to meet me.

"Then I could just buy it for you so that you drink at home."

"I'm okay. Thank you for the offer," I said and took a step away.

"Come on Natasha, why not get some *soya* or roast fish?"

"I said I'm alright," I thundered emphatically.

He asked me to give him a second, crossed the road and dashed to his car. In a split second he was back with something wrapped in a black plastic bag. He handed the parcel to me, but I refused.

"This is some cake for you to crown your evening with."

"I don't eat cake."

"Wow! Interesting, but you can give it to a friend."

"I don't have a friend." Then I scowled at him and said, "Besides, your gifts are becoming a pest."

"No strings attached."

"Then what?"

"I love you, and I just feel like helping you, Natasha."

I looked at him eyeball to eyeball and said, "I'm engaged."

"That's okay, Natasha." He started playing with his car keys. "That's the more reason why I'm closer to you. You are beautiful and intelligent."

"Can I go now, sir?"

"It was a pleasure meeting you again."

He shook my hands and we separated.

As I paced to my room, a wild thought kept pelting me that I should give him an ear. I was drowning in poverty and here was a rich dandy ready to douse me in cash. Perhaps a dalliance with him could give me enough money to take care of myself and foot the bills for my treatment. I started pondering the possibility of going out with him briefly. I knew I was going to protect myself with condoms. No, protect him if he was at all free. But Demas was madly in love with me. How could I betray his unflinching love given that he'd sworn to love me till doomsday. I made up my mind not to renege on my promise of remaining faithful to him till the end of time.

I received a call from a strange number while I was opening the door to my room. I hesitated to answer the call, but as the caller persisted, I decided to receive it. Behold! It was Demas calling. He told me that he forgot his charger at home and had attempted twice but unsuccessfully to call me when the battery was still full. He told me that he had had the worst experience in his life. When I asked him to give the gist of what was amiss, he replied that it was not something that could be discussed over the phone. He told me that he had made the more than one-kilometer journey twice that day to call me. He said the first time he attempted calling, the lines were not going through at all. He assured me that he would leave the following night and arrive in Yaoundé on Tuesday morning.

Just when I finished talking with Demas, Mr. Jonathan called to say he was sorry if he had offended me. He asked if I could meet him at the Central Market by 3 p.m. the next day. I told him that I would be busy. Then he suggested that I should get ready by 8 p.m. the following day because he'd like to take me to a cabaret, but I also turned down this offer. He asked again if he had made me upset. I quickly dismissed him from talking on and on by telling him that he hasn't slighted me at all. He bade me goodnight.

I was restless. I could hear the name Demas…Demas…Demas singing continually in my ears. I needed to see Demas, to hear from him why he had suddenly traveled home. He was not convincing over the phone. What was difficult for him to tell me the truth or simply give me a hint about his mission home? If he no longer had interest in me, he should have told me that his father was forcing a girl on him, but he was standing his grounds. The news of him going home for a wife was beginning to make sense to me. I was gripped by the fear of the unknown and waited for Tuesday with anxiety and apprehension. In moments like the one where I found myself, I began experiencing sporadic headaches and pounding heartbeat. As I lay in bed praying for Tuesday to fly by, the words of Thomas Hobbes in *The Leviathan* that "the life of man is solitary, poor, nasty, brutish, and short" kept hounding me.

EIGHT

My joy exceeded all limits when in the afternoon the next day Demas called me from a phone box and told me that he was about to board a vehicle from the village to Bamenda where he would leave for Yaoundé. The fact that he called me showed that he was still in love with me. Well, he could just be preparing my mind for the bomb blast. However, I spent the entire night singing songs of praise. My stomach discomfort had stabilized. I couldn't believe that I had bounced back to health. My next plan was to consult Pa Bobga, another renowned herbalist, who was specialized in treating sexually transmitted ailments. Maybe by some stroke of luck I could be healed. I had also heard claims that he treated HIV carriers with relative ease. I would not mind using my university tuition for my health. After all, what would a sick and dying person do with a certificate? Herbal treatment was definitely more effective and cheaper on account of the many people turning to it. My major problem was money. I needed to be eating well too because, as Demas said, good medication accompanied with poor eating would amount to nothing

As early as 6 a.m. on Tuesday, I had already trekked to Carrefour Obili, anxious to meet Demas. Normally, all buses that leave from Bamenda by night begin arriving in Yaoundé by 6:30 a.m. But on that day, I was puzzled that not a single bus had showed up by 7 a.m. I strolled to Binam, another sister travel agency, but there were no signs of any bus arrival from Bamenda. By 8:00 a.m., surprisingly, a thirty-seat bus of the Binam agency arrived. It was drenched in mud. Fifteen minutes later a thirty-seat bus from the Amour Mezam agency arrived too. It also was covered in mud. I was horrified when the passengers started trickling out lackadaisically from the bus. They looked rumpled and wrinkled as they disembarked. They were muddier than the bus which transported them.

Demas had told me that he was in a seventy-seat bus. For curiosity's sake I edged closer to the bus door hoping to see him. Demas was not among the passengers. My songs of joy were gradually being turned into songs of sorrow.

The look on the passengers' faces spoke of endless woes. Other relatives and friends who had come for their loved ones including passersby were anxious to get a glimpse of what had transpired on the road. Since I was so concerned too, for obvious reasons, I sharpened my ears to get every tit bit of anguish the weary passengers managed to recount.

"*Economih don pappleh. No roads,*" one passenger, unwilling to talk, just shook his head and said as he plodded away with a bag on his head. It was clear that no taxi could carry him in that filth. I knew that the economy was crazy, and that the roads were bad as that old man said, but I had never seen the like.

At one corner at the bus agency a lady in *kabba* and a twined loin wrapped round her big waist was wailing and bemoaning her fate: "*Govmen noh fix road. Transport and petrol so, so rise. Now my njama-njama bag don loss for sika push push moto.*"

She was a vegetable trader who had come to supply huckleberries to the capital city. Unfortunately, due to the bad roads the passengers had been struggling to push the bus out of mud until one of her bags containing her produce fell off the bus and went missing. Onlookers sympathized with her quietly as they shook their heads, sighed and left.

A teacher who was coming to follow up on his documents

in the ministry of public service took time off to explain to the surging crowd what had happened. He said it rained almost the whole day in Bamenda rendering the already dilapidated and pot-holed Bafoussam-Bamenda road almost impassable. He decried the potholes which have been transformed into gullies and lakes. According to him, they had pushed the bus for hours out of mud before they were able to make it to Santa where the road was a little improved. He made it clear that the situation could not be resolved in the nearest future unless there was enough sunshine in the days ahead. He ended his nightmarish tale by saying that an interminable fleet of cars had lined both sides of the road making it impossible for any car to either leave or enter Bamenda.

"What do you expect when the politicians spend eighty percent of their time out of the country and only come home during campaigns?" a hawker complained before soliciting people to buy his bread.

"My brother, the politicians go abroad to dye their hair or to get medication for headache," another hawker corroborated.

The bread seller put his bread on a stand. "But when they die abroad their corpses are brought here as if Cameroon is a cemetery. Check the investments of these politicians abroad, then you will understand what I mean. I left the university a couple of years ago, here am I."

I could read desperation in the faces of the people who listened to the gory tale. I could see their plans shattered. Some of them needed to travel or needed to see their loved ones. I decided to wait for thirty more minutes to see whether the bus Demas boarded would arrive. After the stipulated time I had set to leave, I still waited for more minutes hoping that a miracle would occur. By 10 a.m. I gave up and went home with the hope of coming back by 4 p.m. When I got home, I dozed off and forgot myself. It was Mr. Jonathan's call that woke me up. The time was already 5:00 p.m. I hurriedly took a shower and then got a bike. Destination,

Carrefour Obili.

The Amour Mezam bus agency looked like a war zone. I expected to see buses, passengers, and relatives or friends, but none of the above was present. I had the impression that I was dreaming. I don't know what came upon me that I had gone to the other side looking for the bus agency across the street. The truth only dawned on me when I looked again to be double sure that I saw the conspicuous signpost of the travelling agency implanted where it has always been, just in front of the building which was the agency's headquarters. I began to develop heart palpitations. I crossed over to the manager of the agency who told me to wait till 6 p.m. He assured me that he had received word that everything was under control and the seventy-seat bus that delayed at Ndikilimiki would soon arrive in Yaoundé.

By 6 p.m. the travel agency was once more full of people who had come for their loved ones. It appeared they had had information to come at that time. At exactly 6:15 p.m. the first bus arrived. It was a seventy-seat bus. I exhaled. I counted the worn-out passengers as they descended the unkempt bus. Most of the passengers were yawning and taciturn as if they were refugees. When the last passenger came out my temperature started rising because he was not Demas. I climbed on the bus but not a single passenger was still on it. Instantly, my mouth became deprived of saliva. I had the sensation of something nibbling around my perineum. My period was due in two days. It was clear that it had come earlier than planned. I had to go home. Luckily a bike was on hand to take me.

When I returned to the bus agency I learnt that another seventy-seat bus had just off loaded. Since Demas's house was not far off, I rushed there. It appeared Demas had just got in because the bags of food he brought lay haphazardly on the floor. He was a very organized man and those bags could not be lying there if he had entered his room ten minutes earlier. I came in when he was struggling to connect his phone to the charger. He embraced me vigorously and lifted me as if we were newly wedded.

"Sorry, Nata... I forgot my charger," he'd forgotten he had told me during his last call.

"I was wondering what went wrong."

"I had tried to call you but network problems..."

"So how did it go... tell me... what carried you to the village?"

"Hmmm... Nata, it's a long story... My father is a case..."

"What did he want from you that could not wait?"

"My father is imposing a woman on me, and he had the--?"

"What?"

Demas creased his face, "Can you imagine that?"

"Demas tell me you're joking."

"In the twenty-first century my father still wants to choose a wife for me."

"But I want to know your stance?"

"What stance?" he asked.

"Demas I'm beginning to doubt you."

"Natasha, if it's a joke you better stop it. I'm not in the mood... you can see I'm very tired..."

"I knew it...," I bit my lips.

"Please if you don't have anything to say you better be quiet."

I left Demas's house more frustrated than I had gone there. I regretted why I was suspicious of him. I realized that I had suddenly become bitter, churlish, and resentful even when someone was doing me a favor. I had quarreled with Clarisse three days ago simply because she asked me to give her a dish to serve me some *ekwang* she had prepared. I had asked her what was wrong with her serving the food in her own plate. Her response had been that if I did not want to eat her food I should leave it. I can't explain the words that shot out of my lips then. "Any way, you know I don't eat tasteless *ekwang*," I had said, "worse still your *ekwang* has neither enough oil nor meat or obstacles." Clarisse just said "thank you" and left my room. I went to her room later and tried to talk to her but she was unresponsive. It took me a couple of hours to reconcile with her.

I knew that Demas was innocent and wouldn't jeopardize his love for me, but I was just being naughty, and foolishly jealous. After the incident, two days went by without Demas coming to my apartment or even calling me. I knew he was furious. I went to his house but he was nowhere to be found. I tried to call him, but he wouldn't answer my calls. I tried calling him with someone else's phone the third day, but his phone was out of connection.

Many thoughts went through my mind. I concluded that perhaps I was right to have suspected him. So, Demas had just left me like that for another girl pretending that his father was trying to hang a woman around his neck. When I contacted Demas's neighbor, she told me that he might have been very busy with his church program and the competitive entrance exams into the Higher School of Mass Communication. This behavior was not typical of Demas. I knew he was preparing to write this entrance examination, but that would never have stopped him from visiting me or at least calling to find out how I was doing.

The next day I went to his house at 11 p.m. hoping to meet him but he was not at home. I waited until midnight but Demas still didn't show up. The following morning, I was at his door. I came in when he was just entering his room. He looked composed as usual. He told me that he had been engaged in an all-night prayer. When I asked him why he was not answering my calls he said he was fasting and did not want anything to infringe on his spiritual life. He told me that his father might go to any length to get him to marry the girl he was imposing on him. His focus on the special prayer was to soften his father's heart and make him abandon the idea. When I listened to him I felt guilty and pleaded with him to forgive me. I also asked him why he didn't ask me to join him in the prayer, but he said he thought I was not in the mood. He had intentionally turned off his phone to concentrate. I felt guiltier after learning of these explanations. My love for Demas was unshakeable.

Each trial moved it to a higher height. The altercation made me even crazier for him.

Before Demas saw me off to my room that day, he told me that Dr. Uma Adebayor, the Nigerian itinerant international evangelist would be coming to Yaoundé under the tutelage of the Full Gospel Mission. Though sisterly Pentecostal churches were involved in the evangelistic outreach, the Full Gospel Mission remained the front runner. He said that the all-night fasting and prayer meeting was mainly in relation to the campaign. This campaign was due in a month's time. So much mobilization was already going on with respect to that. The man of God was a tool that God had used mightily for His glory. The lame have walked, the blind have seen, and the dumb have spoken under his ministration. There were even rumors that the dead have risen thanks to his prayer. Dr. Uma Adebayor has, through the mighty power of God, prayed for many and they had been healed of acute, chronic and incurable ailments. As a mighty Man of God, curses have also been broken through his ministry.

I strongly believed that this preacher's coming to Yaoundé was not by chance. God had intentionally done it to heal me. It was high time I made myself available for the power of God to touch me. When Demas told me about this, I burst into song in his room.

Pass me not oh gentle savior
Hear my humble cry
While on others thou art calling
Do not pass me by

Savior savior savior
Hear my humble cry
While on others thou art calling
Do not pass me by

NINE

A week before Dr. Uma Adebayor's coming to Yaoundé, the city was in a tense and excited mood. I was glad to be part of this edifying and inspiring event given that the All University Games were going on and classes had temporarily stopped. Christians from nearly all the Pentecostal churches in the city mobilized and erected billboards at strategic corners of the city. Both the national and private radio stations were contacted by the sensitization committee. The radio made several announcements with respect to that. As the day of his arrival approached, the advertisements on the national station and private-owned radio and TV stations, which recently joined the cue, intensified. The Christians went wild like locusts. They combed every nook and cranny inviting people and distributing tracts. I occasionally assisted with this. The arena for the grand occasion would be the Amadou Ahidjo Omnisport Stadium.

A few days to the event, Demas mistakenly dropped his phone in a pail of water. He took out the battery, placed it in the sun to dry but to no avail. I told him to take it to a phone repairer but he refused. He said that he would not spend another franc on the phone again. He had already spent more than half the original value of the phone on previous repairs, which had become frequent. He suggested he might buy a new phone in December, which was a few months away, and new designs were expected to be released accompanied by exciting sales.

As days to the evangelistic crusade approached, I became increasingly involved with other activities to make the campaign a huge success. I attended several meetings at the Full Gospel Church at Cradat with Demas. I went to Sunday meetings, Bible studies, prayer meetings, and prayer cells. An incident happened in one prayer meeting that left me humiliated and dumbfounded. I was asked to intone a closing song during one of the meetings. I had no time to reflect on what song to sing. I began clapping and marched in front of the worshippers with these words:

Today maybe the last day you don't know brother
Today, today, today maybe the last day you don't know…

There was stunning silence. I repeated the chorus and the worshipers burst into paroxysms of laughter. I was transfixed for a moment before it dawned on me that the song I intoned was mostly sung at funerals. It was the pastor who came to my rescue by intoning:

Hold somebody
Tell him that you love him
Put your hands together and praise the Lord…

After this incident, I almost did not want to attend the prayer cell meetings again. Demas encouraged me to focus on Christ and not on man because the latter would always fail me. He told me that Christ was the author and finisher of my faith and salvation, and as such should be my only example to emulate. "Man will always fail," Demas lectured me, "All great men of God had their weaknesses, but that did not deter people from practicing their Christianity."

I fasted for two days in order to render my body available for healing. Dr. Uma Abebayor's crusade was not one to miss. I was confident God would touch me during one of the meetings. People had streamed in from different towns and cities with their burdens for the preacher to deliver them.

Three days before the Man of God's arrival, I went to see Demas at his apartment and when I entered, I was astonished to find a girl lying in his bed. Demas was not there. No one needed to tell me who she was. She must have arrived that morning. I saw bags smeared in fresh mud strewn in one corner.

Since I did not suffer a stroke that day, I don't think I will ever suffer a cardiac arrest. When I banged his door behind, all I could experience was a total blackout. However, I managed to stagger to the road since I did not want to stay around his house for the next second. I found it incomprehensible that Demas could be toying with my emotions and something as sacrosanct as marriage. I did not know how and when I reached the main road. Demas had done his worst and the only way to pay him back was to pour acid on him. I was also terribly jealous of the village girl I had met in his room. How could Demas do this to me? What had I done to my God to deserve this cruelty? So man's life on earth was plagued by problems he would never overcome? I knew my immune system would get weakened the more and opportunistic infections would set in soon. I cursed the day Demas stumbled on me and blamed myself for giving in so cheaply to his gimmicks. I was overwhelmed by the downturn of events and my stomach started grumbling as if I would suffer from diarrhea. I tried to mumble a few words of courage to myself but the words choked me. "Why must it always be me?" I sighed and muttered. Demas was my last hope…and now… If ever I had desired death, that was the moment. I wished I could meet God in person to table my plight directly to him. Though life was generally unfair, the vicissitudes of life I had experienced were unbearable. I wished I'd died the day I was born.

As I stood by the roadside waiting for a taxi, my legs continued to dangle as if I were under the influence of whisky or drugs. I could feel my chest pounding like the jaws of a toad. I stopped three different taxis but none of them was going in my direction. I began reeling as if I had just been punched on the face. "Demas…Demas… Demas how could you do this to me at this critical moment?" I heard myself ask. "Is it because of my health that you have decided to treat me thus?" I was lost in thought and self-evaluation that a taxi stopped by and hooted several times with the driver asking me where I wanted to go to without me noticing until a pedestrian nudged me. I came to self-realization as if from a dream. Before I could utter a word to the taxi man about my destination the passengers burst into guffaws as the driver sped off. After waiting for about ten minutes I finally got a bike to transport me.

When I got back to my room my ears were assailed by the sound of Eric Donaldson's "Where is the Love that you have for me?" It was coming from Clarisse's room as if it were a nightclub. This was more than a coincidence.

I entered my room and found a long letter folded like a rattle snake sitting under the door. I knew it had to be from Demas, and I was afraid to read it. I stared long at it as if it were a dangerous snake. This reminded me of his promises of unconditional love. Tears gushed out of my eyes. Demas was a dreadful puff adder with multiple heads. I went to the toilet. When I was finally able to pick it up, I read it with trembling hands and chattering lips. He began by saying that he had tried calling me through a call box phone but to no avail. True, my phone had been down the whole day. Its battery had died. He wrote that he was devastated and heartbroken to discover that his dad had brought the girl—his wife-to-be— all the way from the village to Yaoundé to force on him. The note also indicated that, to his surprise, he had been chosen to take the place of the church's youth leader as one of the delegates to receive the prelate from Nigeria at the Douala International Airport. Demas, accompanied by some church members, was already on his way to Douala to welcome the preacher. The youth leader, who could not accompany them because of other urgent matters he needed to attend to, had delegated much of his powers to Demas. I was not as surprised as he was by the honor. Demas was chosen because of his zeal, eloquence, penmanship, and dynamism.

Demas would return in one full day to explain the details to me in person. I was confused. Who was I supposed to trust? I had never heard of a father forcing a girl on his son to the extent of bringing her all the way from the village to the city. Demas had to have been an accomplice. The truth had finally come out. Pretense and falsehood can never hide. I loathed both Demas and the girl with every fiber of my body. I just wanted both Demas and the girl, or myself, to disappear from the surface of the earth.

I resolved not to set eyes on Demas again. It was even good that my phone battery was completely down. I wouldn't have to listen to his pathetic explanations, trying to convince me that he did not love the girl but was just out to satisfy his father. I would not go to Demas's house ever again and to do everything in my power to stay away from him.

The next day, before the cock crowed, I was at Emelda's room. I spent all day with her and only went back to my room in the depths of the night. The following day, I did same. When I got home, I saw another note just behind the door, obviously from Demas but tore it into shreds without reading it. Why would I read anything from him? I was not interested in his gimmicks. I had outgrown that. He was not worth killing myself for.

I spent that night trying to decide whether to go home to Ndop to tell my parents about my condition or simply stay in Yaoundé. In the end I concluded that it was better I confided in my mother. I was closer to her than my father and she was more understanding. I was going to miss the crusade. The world was full of fake people, and Demas had just proven beyond all doubt to be one. He was even more deadly than any venom because he had been secretly and gently killing me.

The next day was a Friday, I boarded a bus to Ndop in the morning, and by 5 p.m. I was with my parents. They were happy but surprised to see me, given that classes were about to begin at the university. They were also so anxious to know about Demas, for they were impressed with the care he gave me when I fell sick a couple of months ago. They said the mere fact that he gave up his studies to bring me home was indicative enough that he was a responsible man. Demas had truly acted well by bringing me home when I was sick. But what would that amount to after lifting my spirits so high only to dash them into shreds? The more I tried to avoid talking about him the more the topic kept coming up. I told them that I was not feeling so well. I said I suspected migraines. They promised to send me to the hospital for a checkup the next day.

I couldn't find the right moment that whole evening to talk with my mother about my health issues. In the evening, my father went out but I was cooking and my mother was in the living room watching the television. I planned to tell her as soon as I was done in the kitchen. I would give her the whole scenario under the guise that it happened to a classmate. From then I would see her reaction and know how to move forward.

When I finished cooking and sat with her in the living room to eat, she unknowingly started the conversation by telling me that the world was bad. I asked her why, then she told me an experience of hers when she went to the doctor and stood for almost thirty seconds without the doctor noticing her presence. The doctor's head was bowed, and he was in deep thought. When he lifted his head and saw my mother, he sighed and told her that he had just advised five people to do the HIV test that morning and all the patients, including an expectant mother were positive. She ended by saying I should be quite careful because the world was really bad. That was my opportunity to tell her of *my friend's* cruel fate. I told her how this friend of mine was still a virgin, but she got entangled in her mess because she was involved in a ghastly accident and helped the wounded without any precaution.

After listening keenly to my tale, my mother told me that she

really pitied this unfortunate girl, but she blamed her for her foolish-
ness. She said that life was exactly like that; fraught with unpleasant
surprises. She said that those who suffer most in the world were the
good people while the bad people prospered and lived longer and
fulfilling lives. I attempted twice to tell her that I was this friend, but
my mouth was too heavy. Just when I finally mustered the courage
to say it, my father banged at the door and barged in as if he was
running away from a legion of ghosts. That was typical of him. He
would knock at the door so hard, but before someone could answer,
he would fling it open and stroll into the room without uttering a
word to anyone—not even my mother, his wife. He did just that
when I was about to be engaged with a life-changing discussion
with my mother. I resolved to tell her the next day.

After breakfast I went to my room to prepare to leave for the
hospital. While I was still dressing, I heard a thud like the sound
of someone falling down. This was accompanied by a loud cry. I
rushed to my parents' room. My mother was on the floor, writhing
and groaning with stomach pains. The pupils of her eyes were nar-
rowing. My father rushed for a car while I stood with her trying to
do whatever I could to relieve her pain. We took her to the hospital
and after a couple of tests the doctor's diagnosis was that a bacterium
had infected her guts. She stayed two days in the hospital and on
Monday morning she was discharged.

Her situation, coupled with the fact that I had told them I was
feeling much better, had made them forget that I had to go to the
doctor myself. My work in the house proved that I was better too,
given that I did a thorough cleaning of every single room.

I was due to leave that day by 4 p.m. in order to catch the 11
p.m. bus to Yaoundé. My mother had improved although she still
looked fragile. She was in no condition for me to tell her my *bête
noire*. I decided I'd tell her during the Christmas break.

The last day of the crusade was Monday and I was due to arrive
Yaoundé on Tuesday morning. My journey was smooth. I slept most

of the time on the bus. I only woke up at Makenene to eat some plums and ripe plantains. I reached Yaoundé by 6 a.m. When I got home and opened my door, I saw a couple of notes shoved under it written by Demas. Rats and cockroaches had destroyed some of the notes. I tore everything into shreds without reading any and dumped them in the toilet. I had had enough, and my mind was made up.

I regretted that Clarisse was not in to keep me company. I decided to take a rest but found it difficult to sleep. I was restless. Emelda had texted me that classes had begun though timidly. I had a noon class and I was so tired I considered skipping it, but by 11 a.m. I was able to make up my mind to attend. I had to keep moving forward with my life, and the class was important.

Life had tortured and battered me a lot, but what was important for me was to make it to heaven. I had to forgive Demas and his wedded wife and move on. I had also just heard over the radio a couple of days before that the price of antiretroviral drugs was being reduced by seventy-five percent, and I took that as a positive sign. God would not allow His own to beg for bread. Heaven was not a place to miss. Life on earth was temporary and full of heartaches. Demas was not meant for me, or he was, but due to one sad twist of fate, he had changed his mind. I hoped to look for Demas to reconcile with him and to move on. Losing him was not going to stop me from following Christ. I planned to go to his room early the next day to talk things out with him. I could not just dismiss Demas from my mind without at least having a talk with him. As I debated the decision to meet him so that we talk over it and part amicably, another voice kept telling me to just lie low and not bother at all. The voice kept insisting that it should be Demas hunting for me to beg for a pardon and not the other way around.

TEN

After a few days, I was overtaken by a mysterious force—one that compelled me to go to Demas's home. I went in the evening to be sure he would be there. I was shocked to discover from his neighbor that Demas had travelled to his village that morning. I knew at once that it was definitely for his traditional wedding and other things related to his marriage. It seemed every action I took brought me more heartache. I swore for the second time that I would not set eyes on him again because seeing him would only infuriate me the more. I wanted some closure with him, and yet I did not want to liberate him and let him go just like that.

One full week went by without me setting eyes on him or hearing from him. I remembered my phone rang on two different days that week but I ignored the calls because I suspected it was him. Demas had a sugar-coated tongue. Whenever I see or hear him speak, my soul would begin to melt. But I was no longer interested in his flatteries.

That week, I occupied myself with reading, listening to music, and watching Nigerian movies. I also received word that my mother was doing pretty well. I just had to concentrate on my studies. Unfortunately, my memory was failing me. It was no longer as retentive as it used to be. I suffered immensely from wandering thoughts. Demas was the one who helped me with most assignments and even lectures. Now that he was no longer in my life, I had to work extra hard.

One of my lecturers had unexpectedly told the class that he was going to give us a test. On the eve of that day, I went to the university campus at night for studies. Just as I opened my books I began to feel sleepy and tired. Even though I was able to push away my fatigue, I could not concentrate. I was reading a single line countless time. In the end I packed my books and went home.

When the lecturer finally gave his test, I wrote the first paragraph and found it difficult to continue. I tried to recall even the plot of the novel *Emma* by Jane Austen but could not. It was such a simple test because we were asked to show the relevance of the text to a Cameroonian audience. Since I could not remember anything, right down to the characters, I handed in my paper and left the hall. I did not care about the jeers, boos, and catcalls displayed by students. Tears smeared my entire face as I trudged out of the hall, head bowed.

When I arrived home, Demas was leaning on the wall beside my door. He smiled when he saw me but I looked away quickly. I almost went back but it was too late. He said hello and moved to embrace me but I did not respond. I opened my door closing it behind me without offering a word to him. The door squeaked open behind me and Demas marched in.

"Can I talk?" he asked, still standing.

"Demas, what else do you want from me?" I asked.

"The problem with you is that you draw hasty conclusions."

I looked away and said, "Please just leave me alone. You got married without letting me know."

That was when Demas made me feel so ashamed. He explained everything to me, how his father came with the girl he had been telling me about without seeking his opinion. He said he went forward on my behalf to see Dr. Uma Adebayor to lay his hands on him for prayers. He surprised me that he had been to my house twice one night just to make sure he got a piece of my clothes or shoes demanded by the preacher as a point of contact for prayer. Those days surely coincided with the days I went to see my parents in Ndop. He explained to me that ever since the girl was brought to his house he had not spent a single night in his room. And that's when the girl saw that the relationship was not moving forward and would never move forward in the next century. At last she demanded that he should take her back to the village. So, he took her to the village and was back that morning but terribly exhausted to come to my house immediately. He finished his story by saying he was deeply sorry for all I'd gone through because of him.

We embraced and I told him that I was deeply sorry for my poor behavior. For the umpteenth time, Demas assured me that only upon death shall we part. I could not explain the relief I felt after this encounter with my one true love. All doors of hope and splendor seemed to open widely before me after this meeting. Once more he put a smile on my face. He assured me that once he passed his exams into the journalism school, we would get married. I prepared some food and we ate and I accompanied him to his house.

At Demas's house, I suggested to him that it was high time we met Professor Victor Che Richard, the putative oncologist and researcher in HIV and AIDS at his renowned Hope Clinic. There were claims over the national radio and television that he had developed a vaccine for AIDS called Vanhivax. Demas thought otherwise. He said he trusted God for my complete healing, if at all I had any issue. Demas, who had been against redoing the test on the grounds that it was a waste of money, was prepared for another test. I was nervous about doing this at any hospital or health center where crowds will see us. I suggested to him that we should go to a nurse I knew who worked at St. Immaculate Hospital as a lab technician. She would take the specimen and do the test and bring back the result to us.

That evening, we went to Sister Mariam's house and made the proposal to her. She agreed to do it, collected the money for the test, but told us to come the next day for the specimen. The next day I went and she drew blood and told me to come back in a week's time given that it was a clandestine act.

I went to Sister Mariam's house for two weeks consecutively without getting anything concrete. One day she told me the machines were the problem. The next time it was the lab technician at the HIV department that was the problem. At another time she complained that she did not go to work because of this or that matter. After trudging the path to her house for weeks, I finally gave up.

During this time, Demas had been so anxious to know the outcome. Each time Sister Mariam played her cat and mouse game Demas would suggest we go somewhere else to redo the test. At times I would tell Demas that Sister Mariam was not around just to calm him down. The last time I told Demas that she had said the technician would soon analyze the specimen, he took umbrage at my statement. Perhaps, it was because I told him that Sister Mariam, who was to bring the test result, had travelled and would return in a week's time.

Demas creased his face and said, "What do you mean?"

"I think we have to wait for her to come back."

"Hmm…come back? I am no longer there."

"What do we do?" I asked.

He stood and put his hands in his trouser pockets. "What do we do? It's simple. Forget about this so-called Sister and—"

"But we have already paid her."

"Then where are the results?" He placed his forehead on the wall and sighed deeply.

I had never seen Demas this mad. I gulped a cup of water and asked him if he would eat something. He merely tapped his leg and sighed.

"Please, bear with me…just understand."

"That is the more reason why we should go to a different place."

"Give me some time, I'll think of a place."

"You should do that faster."

One sultry afternoon, I went to Professor Che Richard's Hope Clinic without Demas's knowledge. The first day I went to the clinic, I was told that the physician had travelled to Bamenda and would be back in a week's time. After a week, I went back only to learn that he had traveled to the US for an award. This was quite frustrating. His collaborators suggested I do the test while waiting for the doctor so that they could determine my viral load, but I refused. Two weeks later, I went to the clinic again, but the doctor was not back from his foreign mission. Demas was already mad with me that I had categorically refused to redo the test. I was so eager to meet him in person. Meeting him directly, to me, was already part of the treatment.

At last I had the opportunity to meet the reputed researcher. He welcomed me heartily, calling me his daughter. After listening intently to my story about helping the victims of the accident without interrupting me even once, he thoroughly examined me physically, laughed and said that my ailment might have been psychological. He asked me if I had done the HIV test before. I lied. I told him I hadn't taken it, but I wanted to begin treatment without the test. He told me to go and think well before coming back for the test. I appealed for him to begin treatment. He refused. I just couldn't stand the sight of another HIV positive result.

In a month's time, I was back at his clinic. I had decided to take the test again, and I thought he would approve of my decision, but he told me that he wouldn't do it. I was stunned about his sudden flip. This was a test that every doctor or parent would want their patients or children to do in order to be sure of their status, but here I was befuddled by a renowned doctor who was barring me from confirming my HIV status. I insisted that I wanted to do the test until the doctor became infuriated. When I was leaving, he called me back and spoke to me at length, reiterating that my ailment was psychological. This made me finally admit that I had done the test.

He was taken aback by my initial lie. When I told him that the test was positive, he told me to go get the result so that he can see it himself. "However," he said, "gone are the days when HIV was a death sentence; now it's simply a life sentence provided you comply with the treatment. But with the Vanhivax vaccine, you can be completely cured." He also relented and ordered his technicians to take my blood specimen.

When I got home, I attempted twice but failed to look at my test result that I had hidden under my bed. First, I did not want to see it. Seeing it was going to kill my spirits. Secondly there were many things under my bed and the test result was in the trunk which was pushed far away beneath the bed.

I also couldn't bring myself to go back to the doctor. I trusted his machines. They would obviously reveal that I was HIV positive. In that case it would be like peeling off the skin of a festering wound. Having two positive HIV test results was more than a death sentence—one was the actual death and the other was the burial. After thinking long and hard I decided to look for a doctor who would lead me into the treatment without me showing him my test results. I just felt awkward seeing the results with my name bearing the HIV virus. I was prepared to go any extra miles to take medications without revealing the HIV test I'd taken or taking the test again. I needed to seal the lips of any doctor for him or her to accord this treatment. However, I knew that this could not be done without Demas's knowledge. How long was I to hide the endless swallowing of tablets from him? If I contacted a doctor and it worked without his knowledge and he discovered it afterwards, I would be in trouble. Looking back, I think my situation had made me to be shillyshally. Not only did I suffer from mood swings, at times I would take a decision and within the next second, change it. My next assignment was to discuss with Demas about beginning treatment without the test and get his opinion. I knew I could convince him to side with me. But Demas was an ardent believer and his fanaticism could make him insist that only God could heal me. On the other hand, he was a learned man. He would insist that I redo the test, let the doctor see the viral load as to know what dosage to prescribe. In Demas' s heart of hearts, he wanted me to be well. The cost of the drugs was no longer going to be an issue. Thanks to international donors, the prices of the drugs were reduced by seventy five percent making the medications affordable. I believed that in a short while, the price would come down to zero franc.

ELEVEN

I met Demas in the afternoon in his room when he was taking a nap. He told me he had been reading all day and was so tired and hungry. It did not surprise me because his competitive entrance examination was due in a month's time. When he left to freshen up, I started contemplating whether to tell him of my recent plans. I even thought of telling him that I had done the HIV test again at Dr. Che Richard's Hope Clinic. I was afraid that telling him this might make him distrust me or even cause him to believe that I would be the type of woman who would always want to do things my own way.

In the end I decided that I would reach the stream first before crossing the bridge. I checked his cooking pots and discovered that he had boiled some rice but no stew to eat with it. I rushed up the road to a grocery store to get some fresh fish and a few other ingredients. When I came back, he was sitting on his reading table and arranging his books.

I fried some eggs for him so that he could eat with bread while waiting for me to prepare the stew. He tried feeding me, but I refused. I put some food in his mouth, he said, "thank you" and joked that he would never feed me again unless I cheered up and believed that I was well. After relishing his meal, he told me that studying was energy-consuming. He said that it was a fact many people were not aware of. I joked that "bookworms" like him are those who face the pangs of it. He was still trying to read, but I closed the book telling him that the one second he would spend with me would not hamper his success in any way. He laughed, turned on the TV and got into bed. He sat in bed in a Fowler's position and put a pillow on his lap. I told him to put on a Nigerian movie for us to watch, but he instead asked me to tell him about some recent news events in the country and the world. When I could not tell him any, he schooled me on the importance of always listening to the news at least once a day.

Demas told me that he was scared of losing me to a neighbor. I was at a loss. He said the meal was so palatable that when we eventually got married, he would never let a male neighbor taste my food. I laughed out loud. He suggested that we go up the road to Carrefour Obili and share a drink. I was so happy because that would be a good environment to present my case of looking for a doctor to prescribe some antiretroviral drugs for me.

When we got there, he said that sitting outside in front of the verandah was preferable because that would give us ample view of the world. He said that seeing people move about in their daily struggles was therapeutic. He then went on to quote Robert Frost who summarized life in three words: "It moves on." I didn't get his point. He told me to look up the street, especially at the main junction. I did. He then told me that those people who appeared to be happy and so busy were encumbered with problems of their own one couldn't fathom. I smiled and said that the only people who were problem free were the dead. Demas tapped his skull as if trying to rummage something he'd forgotten, and then said, "Aha do you remember 'Friends Beyond' by Thomas Hardy?"

I was ashamed to tell him that I had forgotten even the basic meaning of the poem. I had read the poem in class and had done so for the sake of it. I could not recall the least thing about the poem.

Demas cited characters in the poem like William Dewy, Tranter Reuben, Farmer Ledlow, and Lady Susan who were now resting in the abode of the Lord and free from the world's cares. I did not care so much then about the philosophy behind the poem when we read it in class. I spent my time admiring Demas's profound knowledge and robust literary skills. He analyzed the poem and told me to read it anytime I was free. He told me that the world was a constant battlefront where we fight from the cradle to the grave. Only cowards gave up the fight, Demas seemed to insinuate. This suggestion gave me the opportunity to present my case.

"Then we have to fight my situation," I said.

"Of course, we are already fighting it, and we've won," he replied.

"How?" I asked a dumb question.

"On our knees and by not accepting it, baby." He snapped his fingers and said, "That is not our portion."

I stared at him, sniffed and said, "Dear, the earlier we begin to face the reality, the better."

"Ever since we got that result, I have not been at peace with my spirit."

I sipped my drink, dropped my cup on the table and said, "You better be because nothing can change it."

"Mind your confessions. The Bible states that we overcome the devil by the power of our testimony."

"Then why was yours negative and mine positive…it shows that everything was authentic."

"It doesn't matter baby. The God we serve is a miracle-working God."

"I do not dispute that, but God has given us wisdom to be wise."

He waved his hand. "Whoever the Son of Man sets free is free indeed. You are a new creation in Christ Jesus."

I bowed my head, yawned and said, "That's theology, I want to see this applicable in my life."

"Has it ever occurred to you that ever since we took the test not a hair from your body has singed?"

I stared at him. Afterwards I looked at my body as if to attest what he just said. There was some reason in what he had just said. By now I should have begun suffering from some opportunistic infections. Besides the one time that I fell sick and he accompanied me to my parents, I had not really fallen sick again. What constantly menaced me was headache which I think could be attributed to stress.

Demas then ordered more drinks and some cake. He told me to make myself comfortable when he saw the expression of surprise on my face. To please him, I smiled and then said there is music in desolation. Until then I didn't know whether Demas was merely trying to comfort me or if he was absolutely convinced that I was HIV free. He tapped my back and said, "You're okay my baby."

I shook my head and said, "No man can be comfortable moving on thorns in bare feet."

"Let's keep trusting God." He cut a piece of cake and thrust it in my mouth.

I first shoved his arm aside before taking the piece of cake. "Please I have a suggestion to make. I don't know how you might take it."

"Go ahead as long as it won't infringe on God's law."

"Let's see a medical doctor who could prescribe some antiretroviral drugs for me to be taking."

"Ha, Nata… You will never stop amusing me."

"How?"

"You know it's practically impossible. Besides they must run more tests to evaluate the viral load, if at all you have anything, before putting you on medications."

"We can encourage the doctor by giving him 'something'"

"Please, don't even go into that. God will be angry with us."

He placed his hand on mine which was on the table. "Let's redo the test elsewhere. In that case we can have a base from where to start. I earlier saw it as a waste of resources, but now I won't mind."

"It's not necessary. The die has been cast."

"Don't be pessimistic."

"I am just being realistic."

Demas guzzled his drink, filled the cup and put it on the table harshly. "Only the test will disprove you."

"I have already done it."

When I said this Demas peered at me as if he'd seen a ghost in broad daylight. I could imagine what was going on in his mind. He was surely wondering whether I was actually sane. He trusted me and thought that I could not have done it without letting him accompany me to the place. I believed he saw this as betrayal. He tried to take his drink but mistakenly pushed the cup which fell on the table spilling the content. Fortunately, the glass was not broken. Many people stopped whatever they were doing and stared at us. Some even stood up prompting others who were not aware of the scene to gaze at what was going on. One of the waiters came to our rescue and cleaned the table quickly.

"I'm sorry," I said when all was calm. Demas's head was bowed. I repeated my apology, but he didn't say anything. I then touched his knees. As if waking up from a deep sleep, he wiped his eyes and said, "Nata, I know it's not true." He shrugged his shoulders and muttered, "All right, all right, but how could you have done it without telling me. No!"

"It's true," I said.

"When? Where? No, no, no… I can't believe you," he shook his head violently.

"Believe me."

"Then how was the result?"

I kept staring at my toes. Demas cleared his throat several times, went to the restroom and came back. He fidgeted around, removed his wallet, touched a few items in it and put the wallet back in the chest pocket of his dark blue shirt.

"Tell me you're joking."

"Why would I?"

"Then what was the outcome?"

"I don't know."

"Ha, tell me you're joking."

I did not utter a word. We finally left the bakery without speaking to each other until we arrived at Demas's house. While in his room, he snuggled me into his arms and asked me to tell him the truth. I lied that I was pulling his leg. He told me never to crack such expensive jokes because I meant the world to him. I had placed myself in a quandary. It would have been better if I told him the truth that I'd actually done the test but the results were still pending. I thought that if I retracted my words and told him the truth, he would distrust me the more. Knowing who Demas was, I opted to stay calm. We chatted on other issues. Demas spoke about our wedding with so much enthusiasm that I was wracked with guilt. I kept wondering how he could be so madly in love with someone like me who would definitely infect him, and perhaps make children who would not outlive their infancy. Demas's love and faith seemed untrue and presumptuous.

I thought I could tell Demas that I was no longer interested in the marriage plan. *Oh ye men of little faith*, I heard an audible voice radiating from my soul chiding me.

Demas's exams were at hand. I did not want to do anything that would upset him. He loved journalism like mad. Anything that upset him could jeopardize his success. The competitive entrance exams had not been launched for the past four years. It was not certain when it would be launched again after this session. I needed to support and encourage him in any way possible. After his success I could then tell him that I was no longer going to marry him. By that time, he would be so happy and busy with school that he would forget about me.

I waited for the month to pass. In the meantime, I resolved to look for a doctor who could prescribe medications for me without further tests. To be candid I just couldn't stand to see the positive results again. When I left Demas's house thoughts of going back to Hope Clinic kept pestering me.

TWELVE

One day I went to Bonamoussadi and confided in Dr. Neba who owned Affordable Care Clinic about my predicament. He told me that it was not feasible at all to begin a treatment without proper testing to see the viral load of the disease in me. I proposed giving him some money to do the treatment anyway, but he insisted that he not only lacked the powers to do that, but also that it was against medical ethics. He said it only my CD4 count could determine whether I was eligible for such drugs and the quantity to be administered. He advised that any doctor who prescribed antiretroviral drugs without adequate and authentic tests would be out to ruin me. I laughed, inwardly though, because my life was already ruined. He also said that before I even go to any hospital to get my monthly medications, I had to present my hospital book to the medical personnel indicating my viral load for proper medication and right dosage; and that I would be doing the tests quarterly so as to determine whether to increase or reduce my medications.

"But that is the point I'm struggling to make here," I said.

"I don't get you."

"I mean that I just need a doctor to write to another one stating my condition."

He waved his hand and said, "Things do not work that way because the CD4 might either be higher or lower. This is the determining factor for the therapy."

"I still don't get it."

"I will not be the one to kill you." He stood up and said, "Besides, as I've said, you will have to be doing the test periodically so that the physician can determine whether to increase or reduce your medications, period."

I left his clinic more frustrated. I regretted why I had even gone there at all, more so because I had made my HIV status known to him. Generally, it is said that two people cannot keep a secret. Now that another person knew my HIV status, I feared that the doctor may go around spreading the information. He just needed to tell a single person who knew me. Before I'd realize it, the news would be on everyone's lips—and my parents would know.

The last time I visited my parents was when my mother got sick. When I came back my mother called and said she had something very important to discuss with me. I was terrified. She might have heard of my ailment or she might have seen the manifestations of some of the signs and symptoms in me. HIV infection was like pregnancy that could not hide. No matter how one tried to shield both conditions, everything would eventually be revealed to the world. If my mind did not fail me, my mother was unnecessarily jittery when I shared my friend's purported story with her. I tried to think what could be so important that she wanted to talk to me, but I couldn't figure it out.

It was high time I told her the truth. I went up the road and called her in a call box. I wouldn't beat about the bush again, and anyway, who was to say that she didn't already know and was merely pretending and waiting for me to tell her myself. When I asked her what she wanted to share with me, she began by saying that she was highly disappointed in me for keeping secrets even from her. She said if I were hiding things from people, parents shouldn't be the ones. She said she was my mother and in that case I should be closer to her than anyone else. My heart felt as if it had shifted to the right. So when I asked her what was it she thought I was hiding from her, she said that it was a long story that could not be discussed over the phone. She also said that she was at the market and not a suitable place to talk.

That was another sleepless night for me. I wept the entire night until my eyes were red and swollen. The next morning, they looked as if they'd been stung by wasps. As early as 6 a.m. I called and woke her from bed. She asked why I was hiding it from her given that everyone was already aware of it. When I asked her what I was hiding, she said my performance as cheerleader during the Cup of Cameroon finals. I heaved a sigh of relief as I held my chest. She said my performance brought so much fame to me and even to them that I could not imagine. She told me that she and my father were moving with their heads high up in the sky because of me. She told me that they were given honorary positions and treated with reverence because they have a daughter who could make the president and other dignitaries of the country cheer and clap. Despite all these explanations, I was still at a big loss.

"So, Mama was that the thing you really wanted to discuss with me?"

"Yes, my Queen, my River Goddess—"

"Mama tell me the real thing…oh, I will soon run out of money. Remember this is a call box…"

She then told me that my performance attracted the parliamentarian for Ndop who wanted me to get married to his son in America. She even said my father was so happy about it and that he and the parliamentarian were already great friends. I asked her if the parliamentarian's son was aware of it and she amazed me that my father had sent my pictures to him and he was glad that I was a perfect match for him. She ended her talk with "We are proud of you. Continue to maintain your integrity."

Subsequently my mother started calling me "Americana" and told me to be expecting a call from my father. In a week's time after the discussion with mom, my father called me. He said that since I had already discussed with my mother there was no need for him to go into details. He said that my fiancé would soon be graduating from the University of Yale as a lawyer. He told me that after his graduation, things would be finalized for the marriage. My father had never been so happy in his life. He made several promises to me boasting how I was lifting them up, and that through me he would see America, the Whiteman's land which was just a stone's throw from heaven. He surprised me that through the help of the parliamentarian he had been employed to work in the Ndop Urban Council as an assistant mayor.

My father promised me a decent life and assured me that I would begin to live again better than I used to. He said I was the silver lining in their cloud. He sent me 100,000 FCFA for my upkeep and made it clear that I would never lack again. My wandering thoughts flew to unimaginable directions

My people describe someone in a dilemma as a bamboo strapped on the back of a dog. Yes, I was placed between a waterfall and a cliff; leaving Demas would not be easy if, of course, he meant what he had been saying that he loved me with passion; marrying him would mean that he would be infected and we would never have children who would live to adolescence. Accepting the parliamentarian's son whom I didn't know and didn't love was a big hurdle. I was HIV positive. Who in his right mind would come all the way from America to marry someone like me? Before the marriage, tests must be conducted for sickle cell anemia and HIV. Granted that none of them were done as a sine qua non for the marriage, I would not be able to travel to the US as an HIV carrier. On the other hand, how were my parents who were quite oblivious of my medical status going to react? How was I to break the news to them. If they had an inkling of my ailment that would shatter their plans for me. As I tried to piece these issues together my gall bladder continuously pumped bile into my esophagus. Then I smiled and berated myself for thinking too far. I was madly in love with Demas and even in my dreams I could not give my hand in marriage to another man.

Meanwhile, Demas had been complaining that I had suddenly become reticent. I told him that there was no problem, explaining that he was busy preparing for his exams and that I needed to give him some time to prepare for it well. I added that I was busy with academics too. He was not convinced with my excuses. He said that the reasons I gave were all flimsy because if any woman truly loved a man she would want to see or communicate with him often even if it were for a second. I asked him if he meant what he just said, he went further to say that a woman would risk everything to maintain her relationship with the man she loved. Despite further excuses, Demas still insisted that there was a problem somewhere, even though he could not pinpoint it.

The anxiety of getting married to Demas and bearing children for him made me perform a dumb act. I bought a concoction called "One Hundred Disease Cure" to see if that could cure me. The three bottles of the mixture I bought became my breakfast, lunch and dinner. The dosage stipulated that I had to take a teaspoon three times a day. I was taking a tablespoon six times a day and even at night. Since the herbal concoction was a paste, I wasn't afraid of any consequences linked to overdosage. I mostly lived on fruits during this period because I wanted the concoction to be as effective as possible.

My parents were lavishing me with money on a weekly basis. I was sure my parents were doing this to persuade me to marry the parliamentarian's son, though I pretended to be on the fence with regards to this, given my love for Demas and my precarious health. The mistake I made was that I told my parents I was going to think it over. This surely gave them the impression that I had agreed. At the back of my mind I preferred remaining single than either infecting Demas or making a fool of myself when the HIV test would be done if I went for the unknown lover in America and

I'm proven a carrier of the deadly virus. Since Demas was hardly teaching regularly, I made sure I gave him some money, bought food and prepared it at his place. Ever since he started sensing my indifference, I was scared and never gave him the least chance to suspect me of planning to abandon him.

On the eve of Demas's examination, I went to his house and prepared one of his favorites - rice and stew. He ate until he was afraid he would explode. That day, he took me out for a drink. I was confused but he allayed my worries by telling me that it was not good to study on the eve of an examination especially if one had been studying hard prior to that. He said he just wanted a relaxed atmosphere to free his mind. While at The Gentleman's Club at Carrefour Emia, Demas told me that I was a source of encouragement to him. He said many a time he had wanted to give up on life but could not because he loved me so much. Normally, I would have been the one to tell him this. He was the one who had stood by me when I least expected. He had tried as much as he could to instill hope in me.

At the club, I applauded Demas for his hard work and reassured him that he was going to make it. It was in this relaxed atmosphere that I handed him a success pen. He thanked me heartily and said he would use the pen in the examination. I told him to simply put the pen in his answer booklet and see the magic the pen would perform. He answered that he would do just as instructed. We both laughed and embraced each other. Demas's destiny lay in a six-hour examination divided into two sessions. The first paper began at 8 a.m. and the second at noon since there was an hour's break interval.

We left the calm and cozy drinking spot at 10 p.m. and I boarded a taxi to my room while Demas boarded one to his. I spent some time praying for him before finally retiring to bed. I lay in bed but kept wondering what Demas would do if he failed the exams and, worse, if I were to cancel our marriage plans. Demas might either kill one of us or both of us if such were to happen. He had already buried all his emotions in me and there was no way of withdrawing them.

It was amid these thoughts that I also felt I should make my stance with regards to the planned marriage to the unknown man in America. I really had to devise a subtle way to tell them that I was not prepared to marry the parliamentarian's son whose only name I got was Brandon. My father was a high blood pressure patient. This devastating news could raise his blood pressure. I needed to be extremely tactful. I had to act fast too.

THIRTEEN

In the morning I received a call from a foreign number. I hesitated to take it, but when the caller insisted, I answered. He was lisping so I could only infer what he was saying. The caller introduced himself as Brandon Simbo calling from the USA. My arranged husband. My heart started beating faster. He asked if he was speaking with Natasha. When I said yes, he laughed and said: "Damn it, man. How y'all doing that way?"

"I am ok, thank you," I replied.

"It's fall here," he coughed. Sorry I've got a flu. But it's damn freezing out there like winter man."

"Ashia." I said to sympathize with his ailment.

"What do you mean?"

"I said I wish you get well fast."

"Oh yeah, thanks. The damn flu. I got your phone number from my old man."

"Okay."

"Come on, so what's up baby? How y'all coping with the harsh climate?"

I was too dazed to utter a word.

"You feel me, baby? I guess it's crazy hot in Africa now?" he asked at the other end.

"I'm listening," I responded.

"My Pop has already said so much about you. I got to see your

picture he sent to me. You've got such a big ass baby. I love you baby.
I'll be coming down by summer for the marriage preliminaries."

"Don't you think it's too fast? We don't even know each other.
We haven't even met."

"Hey baby…nothing gonna stop me from loving you. I will
text my email address to you. I got to fly to Virginia now for a
one-week residency."

"Resi what?"

"Residence, my angel."

"Okay," I said without understanding what he meant.

"Hey baby, you got sometime so we can skype tomorrow?"

"No," I answered, without the least idea of what skype meant.

"You must be damn busy that way. Shoot me a text so I can get
your email address."

"I don't have one."

"That's crazy man." He laughed at the other end. "You've got
no laptop?"

"No."

"I will send you some dollars to get one."

"No thank you."

"You damn need it baby. How are y'all coping without that?"

"I'm a bit busy now."

"Yeah, baby we've got to talk some time. Later."

I did not respond.

"Chilly out here, man. Hope y'all are pretty free from bullshit
in Cameroon."

I called my mother after he dropped the call and told her that
I did not love Brandon and would not get married to him. I saw
no reason raising my parents' hopes for something I knew couldn't
work—not even in the next world. My mother was stunned and
remained silent for about a minute before responding. When she
spoke, she was just yelling at me over the phone. She said that
all the marital arrangements had already gone so far that nothing

could stop it. When she heard that I was adamant, she softened her voice and began cajoling me. She pleaded with me to get married to Brandon in order to save face for the family. She said the family was drowning in excruciating poverty and I was about to spurn God-sent manna. When I tried to reason with her, she insisted that marriage was not all about love, but that self-interest also played a major role. She said her forefathers got married to many wives for many reasons like farm work and sexual yearnings. The wives on the other hand accepted because the men were well to do. I told my mother that we're in an entirely different era. This infuriated her the more. She told me to call my father and tell him, and then hung up the phone. I called her again, but she did not answer my call. I went to a phone booth and tried calling her from a different number, but she must have guessed I was the one because she didn't pick up.

I could not for the life of me tell my father that I was not interested in marrying Brandon. The only person who could relay such a message to him was my mother. I decided to give it a day before calling her again. Perhaps by then she would have calmed down and she might listen to me.

In the evening I visited Demas who had just come back from writing his competitive entrance exams. He was frying some eggs. When he saw me, he was so happy and wrapped me in a passionate embrace. He gave me a peck and said I came just at the right moment. I thought he meant to help him fry the eggs. On the contrary he said he wanted to prepare it and call me to come and eat my share. He was happy that I would now eat it warm. When I tried taking the onion he was holding, he told me to sit and watch what a man could do. I was so anxious to ask him how he did on his exams. He said everything was within reach and that he was sure of making it. Except, he said, "You know our country," he clapped his hands.

"But God will always stand by His own," I said.

"A loud amen to that my dear."

"So, when will the results be released?" I asked.

He rolled his eyes and said, "One can't really tell." Upon reflecting he said, "In about six weeks."

"That's really fast."

"The delay in releasing public exams of this nature is always due to corruption-this minister or this director wanting this or that candidate to be included in the list of successful candidates."

"If anyone attempts to keep your name from that list of successful candidates, the Holy Ghost will blind them from removing it."

"Amen...Amen...Amen," he shouted and flipped the egg in the frying pan with some dexterity.

"You're such an excellent cook,"

"Ha. Eat it first before praising me, oh."

When I put the first chunk of egg and ripe plantain in my mouth, I found it irresistible and I exclaimed, "*Uummh...* men are truly better cooks."

"You mean it?"

"This is the least I could do."

The next day I called my mother, but she was still seething with anger. She told me that this was the opportunity of a lifetime and I wanted to let it slip off my finger and deprive the family from living a good life. She said that any girl would readily marry Brandon just by the flip of a finger. She bemoaned her fate wondering why her situation was always different. She lamented that I was removing food from my parents' mouths, arguing that I had refused to eat with kings and princes and instead preferred to pick crumbs from the soil. When I tried talking to her about Demas in order to see her reaction, she told me to get married to Brandon and leave for America so I could create space for Demas to meet another girl. When I told her that America did not interest me at all, she exclaimed and said "*Eish* look at my fool." This made me burst into laughter. She said that she knew that I was merely joking. She encouraged me to come home after my second semester exams to meet Brandon's father because he was anxious to see me.

"Mama I'd already told you I'm not interested in it all."

"Then what interests you?"

"I've already told you, I don't love Brandon, or whatever you call him."

"Listen to her. Why are my own things always like this? You will not be the one to kill me Nata."

"Kill you, Mama? It hasn't come to this."

"Not marrying according to your parents' wish is homicidal."

"Please, Mama, help me tell Papa," I said emphatically.

"You better learn to blow your own fire," she said and hung up.

FOURTEEN

A week after arguing with my mother, my father called me to report to Ndop because he had an important message for me. When I suggested to him to wait until I finished with my second semester exams, he said it was urgent.

I had to travel by the weekend and return by Sunday. There was nothing to convince me that my mother had not talked to my father about our recent discussion and my stance. I boarded a bus that Friday night fearing for the worst.

I arrived Ndop on Saturday morning. My father had accompanied the parliamentarian to Bangolan to campaign against the next parliamentary election. I was surprised that my father had suddenly become a politician and was busy traveling from place to place canvassing votes for Brandon's father's reelection. I waited for him all night to return because I needed to leave on Sunday since I had a revision class on Monday. My father was hardly out after 10 p.m. I waited for him until 11 p.m. but he did not show up. By 11:30 p.m. I lay on the couch in the living room and finally passed out. He woke me up at 12:40 a.m. complaining that the roads to Bangolan were nearly impassable. I thought it was ironic that they were going to woo the electorates but could not even grade their road so as to give the electorates access to their farms.

He pleaded with me to go to bed. The discussion could wait until morning. When I agreed, he patted me, yawned and dragged himself to his bedroom. My father was never used to pleading with me for anything. He simply dished out commands.

It was another sleepless night for me because I still kept thinking about what he had to discuss with me that could not wait or be discussed over the phone, and now it could wait until morning. By 6 a.m. I was set to travel back to Yaoundé. I was already in the living room waiting for him. My mother had gone to the market to buy some foodstuffs for me since it was a market day. One hour later he showed up praising me that he was a wolf that had given birth to a tiger. I was at a complete loss. He hugged me several times before letting me sit down.

He began by telling a long and boring story of how hope was almost lost for the entire family until my star shone for the world to see. He said there were plans he could become the next mayor with the backing of the parliamentarian. I asked him the reason for my urgent visit. He said it was for me to take some essential documents to the US Embassy in Yaoundé in preparation for my trip to America. He said my mother had already discussed everything with me, so he wouldn't waste his time on that. He told me that he and Brandon's father had watched the video countless times on my brilliant performance during the Cup of Cameroon. The plan was that the earlier I left the country, the better, because Brandon's father had overheard the governor's remark of marrying me to his son.

"You know our tradition, my daughter," my father said.

"What, Papa?"

"Our family cannot marry someone from another village."

I giggled then went silent.

"Mr. Brandon has a wonderful career before him, and I think you will make a wonderful couple."

When I told my father that I was still thinking it over because I did not have an iota of love for Mr. Brandon, he stood and told me that there was nothing for me to think about. He said his word was final, that whether I was comfortable with the deal or not, I

must marry him. So saying, he pulled out some brand new crispy
bank notes from his chest pocket and handed them to me. He gave
me some documents to certify in Yaoundé. He also gave me some
money to do some tests, among which were HIV and tuberculosis.
When he went into his room, I counted the money. It amounted
to 150,000 FCFA! The documents to certify cost much less than
that amount.

While at the bus agency my mother asked me if it went well
with the discussion I had with my father. I told her that all did not
go well. She said I won't be the one to send them to an early grave
and left the bus agency. This was the first time my mother had ever
left me like that. I just could not make myself love Brandon. Demas
was my soul mate. I had never known Brandon and he had never
known me. Everything being equal I would prefer to die in my
poverty than to marry him. Besides, I was HIV positive.

It was already close to a year since I was declared HIV positive.
Back in Yaoundé, Demas kept pestering me to go for an HIV test
elsewhere that could produce genuine results. He assured me that I
would be amazed with the outcome. I shook my head. "Trust God,"
he smiled as he said this.

"I thought at one time you did not want me to do the test."

"Right. I saw it as waste, but now I want you to confirm the
negative result. I know that has been your bug bear. This will dispel
any iota of fear lingering in us. My spirit is at rest dear. I have never
been at peace with myself about any issue like this."

By this time, just a couple of months after my fate was declared,
clinics doing the test had sprouted in the city and the country at
large. At last we went to the Etoug-Ebe Health Center owned by
the Baptist Church for the test but luck did not smile on us that
day because the delegate for health for the Mfoundi Division was
due to visit the health center, so it wasn't attending to patients. To
aggravate the situation, specimens were collected in this health
center only on Tuesdays and Thursdays, since it was the last day

of the week to collect specimens, this meant that we had to come back the following Tuesday.

On Sunday, August 19th after the church service, I decided to take a nap as I've been doing lately to drown my sorrows and frustrations. After a couple of minutes, I heard, as if from a different planet, a bang on my door. I shook off the prowling horns of slumber. After a few seconds, the knocker banged again harder. I screamed at who was whamming on my door in that manner. Demas answered softly that he was the one. I flipped the door open. He stopped sharply in the doorway with an expression of incredulous horror on his face that I've never forgotten up to this day. I asked him if he was all right, but he simply stared at me and twitched his lips. I saw his knees sag as if he'd received a knockout blow.

"Please, I hate to see you like this.

"I received some bad news," Demas mumbled.

I supported my frame on the wall, "Where, what, when…? I mean what happened? Who told you?"

He took in a deep breath. "My mother called—"

Is she all right? Anyone sick or—"

My father had an accident."

Where? Is it serious?

Demas bit his lips and cracked his knuckles. "In the bush?"

I adjusted myself. "In the bush?"

While still standing, he said, "My mother told me that my father was returning from the farm and had accidentally stuck his leg in a locally fabricated trap for small game. He is currently at the Banso Baptist Hospital under intensive care."

"Oh God why at this time?"

He sniffed. "I have to leave as soon as possible to go attend to him."

In teary eyes, I yelled, "Life offers bitter blows. Why nah, why at this moment?"

He patted my back and said, "God is with us and He will surely see us through."

"Have you realized that ever since I knew you, we have been jumping from one mishap to another?"

He dabbed my face with a handkerchief, held my hand and said, "Baby, this is not the time to apportion blame."

"Why won't I?"

"Haven't you heard that nothing good comes easy? Only the test of fire produces fine gold. I know that soon we will be out of this mess."

"I pity you. The journey will be rough because of the bad roads… and you will have to spend sleepless nights at the hospital."

"God will take care," he said while patting me.

Demas did not have enough money on him, so I had to use part of the money my father gave me to foot his travelling expenses and for his upkeep while with his father. Since it was during the raining season, Demas left the keys to his room with me so that I could keep an eye on his belongings.

My face remained cloudy the whole day after I saw Demas off at the bus agency in the morning the next day. "Be strong for me," he'd said while tapping my back.

I had smiled and retorted, "God's in control."

"Amen," Demas had clenched his fists while saying this.

"I don't think I will be able to bear your absence."

Demas had squeezed my hand tightly and said, "I will be with you in spirit."

"I hope," I had said with tears welling up in my eyes.

When the bus finally left, it seemed as if part of my soul had gone with it. I dabbed my eyes with a disposable handkerchief. As I lumbered home, I kept wondering how I would cope without Demas. He had stood by me in rain and shine. I needed him more than ever before to continue to muster hope in me even though I was forever damned. I planned to intensify my prayer for Demas's father so that God would speed up his healing. I would be indoors most of the time interceding for both Demas and his father.

A few days later after his departure, my father started pestering me to send him the results of the medical tests he had asked me to do.

"Papa I will send them," I said when he woke me up from sleep one morning.

"You children of today, I don't understand you anymore. A simple thing you cannot do," he screamed over the phone.

I pretended as if I did not know what he meant, "What have I done Papa?

"What does it take to obey simple instructions and do a simple test? I had given you enough money and I have been waiting and waiting…If you know the importance of—"

"But Papa I had said I will—"

I could hear him clear his throat and spit out. He then shouted, "So you've not done it? What's going on? It's taking ages. Can't you see? You want to miss this golden opportunity? Your husband's father brought me some wine, jackets, and even some tablets from America sent by his son to him for body pains. Just one tablet treats—"

I was becoming agitated. I stomped my feet on the floor, "Papa… Papa why all the lecture?"

"Try and send the test results to me this week unfailingly."

"I will see Papa."

When he hung up I became so downcast. Though Demas had encouraged me and even assured me that doing the HIV test again was just a formality and a means of assurance to me that all was well, I still did not have the courage to do it. What if the results show HIV plus, plus? I asked myself.

Later that day, I was beginning to cave to my father's demands to do the test. Doing the tuberculosis test was no big deal. This time around there was no escape. I had to do the HIV test and send the result to him as soon as possible. However, I was not ready to do the test again for obvious reasons. My entire life had been dominated by fear and by "what ifs". Doing the test was only going to drown me further. It would remind me again, even stronger, that I was a walking corpse. Finally, I decided to go to Mokolo market, the most populous market in the city, to distract myself with eye shopping.

It is really true as they say that necessity is the mother of invention. I did the tuberculosis test but did not have the courage to do the HIV test. A single moment did not go by without me thinking about what to do about the HIV test. When I came home that day, exhausted after walking the length and breadth of the vast market, many thoughts flashed on my mind. I should just damn the consequence and tell my father that it was needless wasting money on a test because I was not the least interested in Brandon. The only thing I had bought from the Mokolo Market was bitter kola to ease my frequent indigestion. I peeled the smallest bitter kola and threw the entire nut in my mouth. Its bitterness made my face splotchy.

I thought of telling my father that I was HIV positive and that only the grace of God and Demas's love have been keeping me alive and making me appear seemingly strong. Whatever decision I took would be like tying stones on a drowning man. That evening, I prepared my best food—*water fufu* and *eru*. The *eru* was loaded with palm oil, meat or "obstacles" as some call it, and pepper. I also chose to be indoors. After eating to my fill, I indulged into wandering thoughts. I could see my rejected remains abandoned in the streets to rot. Then by some turn of events I saw myself happily wedded to Demas. I imagined myself being whole again like the lepers Christ healed. "Wow…wow…wow… my joy will know no bounds," I exclaimed.

The next day I stayed indoors lost in thought. It was during one of my absent-mindedness that an idea came to mind—Demas's test result obtained at Klongkak. A name swap after scanning the document could do the magic. I began jubilating only to realize that it was not feasible given that the test had been done months back and it bore Demas's three full names—Demas Lambi Nyuisho. My father was persnickety and would scrutinize every letter or figure found on the paper bearing the test results. In the middle of the night, the movement of rats in my trunk under my bed woke me up. I tried to fall asleep again but could not. I decided to sit at my reading table and think of a way out. The room looked haunted. My clothes on the stand hung like scarecrows. The chiming of my little wall clock echoed in my ears like the toll of my funeral bell. The noise of a dog growling and another made by the exhaust pipe of a motorcycle far away made the room scarier. I jumped back to my bed and wrapped myself in a blanket despite the heat.

I had to figure out what to do in order to satisfy my anxious father. I had heard that in Bonamousssadi where the university students resided, any document could be forged or fabricated. Such documents looked as authentic as their real counterparts. But another option came to mind—to make it more authentic, I would take Demas's test result where someone would merely scan the paper, change the name and both dates on the paper. The next day by 6:30 a.m., I was in Demas's room scouring it like forensic experts. Given that his room was not overstuffed with junk, I believed it would take me less than no time to fish out his HIV test result. It turned out that I was looking for a pin in a haystack. First, I went to his files neatly placed in his bookshelf, but the much-needed document was not in any of them. I opened his two boxes but was not lucky. I went to his trunk loaded with photocopies and wasted about an hour there. I took down all his clothes from the stand and placed them on his bed. I checked one after the other but the paper bearing his HIV test result was not there. I was hungry but decided to try one more place—his mattress. When I lifted the mattress, I picked up a file from under it. I opened it hastily, but it contained only his transcripts. I started wondering whether he had taken the test result to Banso Baptist Hospital too. I was exhausted and went up the road to get myself a loaf of bread and butter mixed with chocolate. After eating, I embarked on the search again. I opened virtually every book of his more than 200 collections, but the document was not in any of them. My forehead had started pounding. I decided to lie in his bed for a while. When I woke up, I lifted up his rug but only cockroaches were running helter-skelter. I gave up. When I was about to leave, I started cleaning his reading table to clear the crumbs of bread I had littered the table with. In the course of lifting the tablemat, a neat envelope in a half sealed transparent paper caught my attention. That was the paper I was looking for. I had taken more than two hours looking for the test result. It was carefully placed in a transparent plastic bag which looked like a file. The paper was as crispy and sparkling clean as it had been handed to us that fateful day. I became envious of Demas when I saw his results again.

The following morning, I was at Bonamoussadi parading the main road that ran through this "heart of darkness," purported to be the students' residential area. The first documentation center I went to did not have the scanner. My heart began pounding in my chest. In the second one, the trainee was willing but could not do it due to inexperience. He attempted twice, failed and gave up. I went back to my room, spent some time reflecting on my plight and afterwards came back to Bonamoussadi. An idea came to mind that I could try a documentation center behind Rose Bowl pub—a makeshift pub of which part of the building was rented out to university students. We haggled the price and settled on 10,000 FCFA. After several attempts with the guy's waste basket almost full of shredded papers, he finally came out with one that looked authentic. When I went home with it, I was not quite satisfied for fear that my freaky father could discover it.

I went back to the guy who had produced the fake document. He was at first reticent. When I insisted that he should give back my money, he almost created a scene by speaking at the top of his voice: "I have delivered the service. Period," he said as he waved his hand to my face.

"But I'm not satisfied."

He laughed mirthlessly and said, "That's your personal cup of tea."

"I don't want it anymore."

"So be it."

I lowered my voice, "Please let's settle this thing amicably."

He frowned, "Settle what?"

"Can you take off 2,000 from what I gave you for your time and give me back—?"

"No way madam. *Go tie juju cam tekam*," he said and concentrated on typing.

I plodded closer to him, "Please—"

"Don't go there…you want me to ex—"

I did not wait for the hammer to land. "It's ok, it's ok," I said and turned my back on him.

When I stepped out, I then chose to go with the dare devil option. I combed every crevice of the jungle called Bonamoussadi and after barely two hours thirty minutes I was back in my little room with a test result showing that I was HIV negative. Even though I spent 15,000 FCFA to get it, I thought it was worth it. I rushed to a nearby off license and got myself a fresh bottle of Top Grenadine to compensate myself for the efforts and success.

When I had drunk more than half of the soda, I scrutinized the paper but found out that it looked more fake than I had imagined. The purported doctor's signature resembled the scratches of a hen's talons. The letters and the words that were deleted and retyped did not match at all. I tore the paper into shreds and dumped it in the dustbin behind my house. I had to do something and fast too. The next day I cornered someone but told him a lie that a friend who is HIV positive needed a medical certificate to travel to Denmark. He linked me to somebody at Bonamoussadi who proposed to scan the document and replaced Demas's name and date of birth with mine for 25,000 FCFA. My plea to reduce the amount yielded no results because he assured me that he would do a perfect job. He asked me to pay all the money before he could begin work. When I paid the money, he told me to come for it in two days. I did not know what I would do if he were to squander my money and not do the job. I could not raise any alarm because I would be incriminating myself. The two days I was asked to come back glided slowly with me spending sleepless nights.

The day I went to collect the paper, only his apprentice was in. He assured me that his boss would come in at most in ten minutes. I waited for 30 minutes but he did not show up. I called him several times but he did not answer my call. Demas's test result was with him. In case he did not show up, what was I going to tell Demas, and what was I going to present to my father or tell him? I started developing a temperature. By 11 a.m. the fever had metamorphosed into full blown delirium. I began sweating all over my body. Just when I was about to leave the documentation office, he came in and apologized for being so late. I was amazed when he handed the paper to me. According to the result, it was done at the medical teaching hospital, and duly signed by professor P. N. Mbarga. Nothing had ever looked more authentic. I gave a thousand francs to the young man as tip. I tucked the HIV test result in my inner wear, thanked him and jumped out highly spirited. The next day, I mailed the HIV and the tuberculosis test results to my father.

Within this time Demas had been calling when the opportunity arose to give me feedback on how things were going. I could not call him since he had no phone. He said his father's condition was improving, but that his right foot just a little above the ankle was almost severed from his leg. He said his father would be in the hospital for at least six weeks. I had to send him more money for his upkeep. I had already used almost everything my father gave me and was barely left with what to survive.

When my father got my test results he called and congratulated me on being healthy. He said he could not be prouder of me and encouraged me to maintain the result and said that it was a good sign that things would work well and I would go to the US.

He addressed me his mother, the name he used to call me when he was happy. "Nchunwa, I can never be prouder of you."

I winced at the other end. "Thank you Papa."

"Through you, your mother and I would one day fly in the plane to take our two eyes see the Whiteman's land."

That was when I told my father categorically that I was not interested in the marriage. He was mad at me and said that I have forfeited any further allowances from him. To restore it, he had bellowed, I must accept to marry Brandon.

"Gone are the days when parents looked for husbands for their children," I made my point at a certain moment in the discussion.

"You either get married to him or you forfeit your allowances."

"So Papa you don't even care about my feelings?"

"What feelings are you talking about when both parents are in accord?"

"Marriage is about couples and not about in-laws."

"Natasha," he shouted, "since when have you become a marriage counselor? What do you know about marriage? You either take what we tell you or you live to regret.

I sat quietly at my end.

"Have I made myself clear?" he asked.

"I remained silent."

"You better do what we are telling you or else—"

He dropped the call.

A week went by with him speaking to me in monosyllabic tones. I thought he was joking. At times he claimed he was too busy and couldn't talk, telling me that he would call. But he never called. After a while I asked him for money, but he told me outright that he did not have a single franc for me. My rent was due in two weeks. I knew that come what may, he would at least send that.

As for food, I became quite frugal. I prepared a meal twice a week. Most often I ate in Clarice's house or at friends' and acquaintances.

When Demas left the hospital with his father and went to the village, he called and informed me that he would be with him for at least three more weeks. The results for the competitive entrance exams he took were still pending. At least, this would have put a smile on our faces. Poverty was already taking a great toll on me. I had visited friends until I was ashamed that I could be nicknamed The-Seen-Guest-At-Every-Meal. I wished Colletta were around to salvage me from this wretched condition.

One day Brandon called and proposed to send me some money through Western Union, but I refused. I made it clear to him that I was not going to marry him even in the next bazillion years. He tried calling me a couple of times after I'd made my stance known to him, so I did not answer his calls. I learned that he then communicated with his father about my intentions, who contacted my father. My father put more pressure on me, but I did not bulge.

The devil knows when to strike. It was at this time that his wiles became more enticing. Mr. Jonathan was not giving me any breathing space as he kept promising heaven and earth to me on condition that I succumb to his carnal urges. Just a couple of days ago, he transferred 10,000 FCFA worth of credit to my phone. I saw it as courting hell and immediately told him to leave me alone. I told him that I was not interested in his antics and that he was not my type. I thought these acerbic words would send him away, but he persisted.

One evening, I sat in my room wondering what to eat. I had exhausted all my resources and there was no one to go to. To exacerbate the situation, Clarice had travelled with her fiancé to the Limbe beach. That day I had drunk water to help with my hunger until the therapy was no longer of any help. I had tried to sleep but my stomach kept grumbling for want of food. It was at this time that Jonathan paid me a visit and offered me 100,000 FCFA, which

I rejected and sent him away with curses. That was how I put a stop to his cajolery because after that he never called me again.

Demas still had three days to be back. I wished he could return faster.

FIFTEEN

At last, Demas accompanied me to Etoug-Ebe Health Centre on May 12 where we both did the test. One week later, on the day we were supposed to go for the result, fear gripped me; I refused to go and told Demas to go and collect it. When he arrived, the counselor refused to release the results without my presence. Demas told me that the counselor said he needed to talk with me because it was confidential. This made the writing on the wall so clear. My heart dropped to the pit of my duodenum. It took Demas two days to convince me to go with him before I reluctantly agreed. I was visibly trembling all along.

I trudged to the counselor's office, who doubled as the health center's chaplain, as if I were going to be decapitated. The counselor, who looked very stern, greeted us with so much formality. He unfolded the papers that contained both results and placed them before us and gave a lecture on HIV, which to me was unnecessary. Though the papers with the results lay clearly before him, none of us could see them because of the soft couches we sat on. I strained my neck several times to decipher what was written on the papers but could not even distinguish Demas's own from mine.

After his tirade, he asked us whether he should begin with Demas's or with mine. I said Demas and he smiled but said ladies before gentlemen. When he saw that I had turned blue, he said he would obey my wish by beginning with Demas's. As expected, he was HIV negative. When the counselor looked at the paper that bore my results, he shook his head and frowned. He then waited for about a minute to elapse without uttering a word. Many deadly thoughts flashed over my mind in a split second. The most salient one was suicide.

When I lifted my head up, the counselor was standing before me and stretching his hand towards me. At this point he had not yet said anything. My body was vibrating. Since I was not sitting far from Demas, I could hear his heart thundering. After the handshake, the counselor went back to his seat, peered at the results again and then said, "I am proud of you, beautiful young lady."

I took in a deep breath. I began feeling tremors on my chest. Tears flowed down my cheeks. I shook my head and blinked several times to be sure I was not daydreaming. The counselor brandished both papers containing our negative HIV test results. I dropped from my seat to the floor before getting up. I turned to look at Demas, but he was frozen in his seat like a statue. Only his lips were twitching. "Thank you, lord…thank you, lord…" He was surely in some kind of trance.

Suddenly, he jumped and embraced me while yelling "P-r-a-i-s-e the l-o-r-d!" I fell backwards, causing a commotion. Nurses and patients scampered to the scene to see what was amiss. When the counselor told them that it was a piece of good news, they went away. Some of the nurses encouraged us to continue to maintain the HIV negative status.

I was still in doubt and disbelief as I stood with my mouth agape.

"Possess your possession," Demas shook me.

"How far are—"

"*Shshpp*," Demas literally closed my mouth with his hands. "Do you doubt God? I told you not to give up."

Demas held my hands and we went down on our knees to pray. The counselor joined us in prayer. In the end he advised us on the different methods HIV could be transmitted and on how to remain HIV negative. He cautioned us to walk in the counsel of the lord rather than in the way of the ungodly.

On the way home we looked at the results several times to be sure there was no mistake anywhere. We were so excited that we shared the good news with the people in the taxi we boarded. I was still happy but not fully convinced. Why was the first result positive? Perhaps the clinic did not take the full specimen, or something went wrong somewhere. I thought of the other test I did at Hope Clinic and deemed it necessary to go and check. I confessed to Demas about the test though afraid that he would be infuriated, but he was rather happy. We immediately hired a taxi to the clinic. When we arrived there, we discovered that we were quite unlucky. They had closed just about five minutes earlier and it was on a Saturday. So, we had to wait for 48 more hours.

While in Demas's house he kept telling me, "I told you...our God is a miracle-working God..." We spent some time worshipping and praising God. I just could not resist looking at the paper containing the test results again and again. At times standing by the window and tracing the words HIV Negative" with my finger. Afterwards I told Demas that I still had some lingering doubts but he dismissed them by telling me that I should be optimistic, and that it was only in the words of our testimony that we easily overcome the devil—the accuser of the brethren. I did not really know whether God had miraculously healed me of HIV-or there was a mistake somewhere, or perhaps the hundred disease cure was the panacea that worked the magic.

On Sunday, I accompanied Demas to church. Even though the church was jammed to capacity, one could easily distinguish my shrill voice during choruses and offerings. I danced during the offertory until I stole the show. I was only short of Geoffrey Chaucer's Wife of Bath in that I was genuine. After the church service, the choir mistress enlisted my name as a choir member, telling me that I will be singing the alto.

As early as 7 a.m. on Monday, both Demas and I were at the gates of Foundation of Hope Clinic. It was only at 8:30 a.m. that the gates to the clinic were flung open to the public. We marched in with expectation and doubt. We were asked to wait because the doctor was not yet around. He was the only one to declare the results. We waited until 9:30 a.m. but he did not show up. I was already hungry. When I complained to Demas of acute hunger, he too said he was in dire need of food. We rushed to a restaurant nearby and devoured some *boboloh* and *mbongo chobi*.

When we came back, the doctor had arrived. There were a few patients he had to attend to so we had to wait. After waiting for about an hour, which seemed like eternity, we were called in. The doctor could not remember me because of his age and due to the many patients he had consulted that morning. When I explained my previous encounter with him, he immediately called one of his workers to bring my medical test results.

Five minutes later the nurse had not come. The doctor rang the bell, but the nurse came and said he had not seen it. The doctor delegated the responsibility to another nurse who came back to give the same report. The doctor checked in his medical records for the technician who collected my specimen that day, then came back to tell us that he was not in the country. He was Mr. Anthony who had travelled to South Africa to attend a seminar. The doctor decided to look for the results himself. Since it was in the opposite room that had a transparent glass barrier, we could see him in his goggles sweating under piles upon piles of files. Other nurses accompanied him. One of the nurses even told him to leave it under her care but he refused. Painstakingly he was going through file after file. I was smiling on one side of my face but sad at the other. After about ten minutes, he smiled and shouted that he had found it. He said the mistake was that when the result came in, it was not recorded—a dreadful mistake made by the attending secretary.

The doctor told Demas to stay out for a while so that he could respect my privacy by delivering the results to me alone. My heart shifted to the right side of my chest when he said this. I thought that the news was so bad that he did not want another person, not even my future husband, to learn of my predicament. However, I told the doctor that I would wish Demas stay. That was when the doctor asked if Demas was my brother because we resembled each other. When I told him that he was my future husband, he ripped the envelope containing the result open and smiled. He then looked at me again; addressed me as his daughter and told me that all was fine.

He recalled that I had once told him that I had done the test elsewhere and it was positive. He asked if I'd checked it as promised, I said I hadn't. He told me that he trusted his machines and technicians. He handed the paper to me containing the result and wished us good luck. I can't explain my joy and Demas's when we left the clinic. We stopped at a bakery, drank some soft drinks and bought some cake. Demas suggested that we should go to my room and compare the two negative test results with the positive one.

While in the taxi, a discussion ensued among the passengers about the dismissal of the director of the Advanced School of Mass Communication. We were stunned about the news because he was such a well-liked and easy-going man. Ever since he headed that institution, most of the students who went to the professional school did so on merit. Proof was the fine breed of journalists who graduated from the school during the director's tenure. Stories had once filtered around that ministers, directors, and other top-ranking government officials had written petitions against him several times for not doing a good job. The real reason for their complaints was that he did not comply with their illicit demands. This time around they wanted him to submit the results of the students' tests to the minister for communication before they were released. There, the powers that be would include their own, possibly unqualified, candidates while the names of successful candidates would be deleted.

The news we got was that he was fired that morning for releasing the results of successful candidates into the Advanced School of Mass Communication without conferring with the minister of communication. Demas had always been keen on listening to the radio and the television for the slightest news but because he went to the clinic with me early in the morning, he missed this latest news As the taxi coursed through the bumpy half-tarred narrow roads, meandering through high traffic, we saw people crowded around newspaper stands. We suspected they were reading the latest news events in the country. We were so anxious to know about Demas's results. We asked the taxi man to drop us. After paying the fare, we went to one of the newspaper stands. Most of the papers were in French and carried headlines of the released results and the sacking of the director of that prestigious institution. Demas bought two of the papers. None of them contained the names of those that had made it.

We boarded another taxi hoping to get a full version of the disclosed results around Melen - an Anglophone fiefdom. But even there, no newspapers carried the names of successful candidates. We went to the journalism school at the Ngoaekelle campus. Many students were crowded before the notice board which harbored the results. Some people were jubilating while others were crying. It took us some jostling and stepping on toes to get through the mammoth crowd to peep at the notice board. Shockingly, some of the papers had been torn by students. So, both Demas and I were left in suspense. More students who came to check their results also expressed a feeling of despair when they discovered that most of the papers bearing the results had been tampered with.

When we were about to leave, someone told the crowd that the administration was about to repost the results. We came back and waited for about thirty minutes before some four men came out with piles of papers and asked us to move behind them if we wanted the results to be put on the notice board. Nobody budged from their standing position. The people shuffled their feet as if to leave and, instinctively, we all moved behind. One of them told us that to make it easier, they would share the papers and post them on different corners. Since the four officials were pasting the results at once at different sections on the wall we decided to trail from person to person since each of them carried just part of the results. When the first official put up part of the results, Demas's name was not among those who had succeeded. We scrutinized the papers again in case there was a mistake, but his name was not there. We moved to another wall and luck still did not smile on us. We had forgotten that the results were alphabetically arranged, pending the orals before the final results would be arranged in order of merit. I could see Demas's pupils dilating. I urged him to follow me to the next wall. He followed me reluctantly, like a goat. When we got there, he refused to look. I traced the paper from top to bottom and from bottom to top but his name was nowhere to be found. He told me that we should go home, but I literally pulled him to the fourth place. The first paper contained his name! Demas collapsed in my arms.

SIXTEEN

We raced to my room in jubilation. The news we just got over the radio was that there would be no oral part of the examination and that those that had made it would begin classes in a fortnight. Demas had just succeeded to begin his dream career. I had just been declared by a renowned doctor that I was HIV negative. I had two results which showed that I was HIV negative and one which clearly stated that I was HIV positive. The elementary math I knew then told me that a million positives plus one negative gave a negative. That was where my problem lay. When Demas saw that I had suddenly become gloomy as we stepped into my room, he nudged me and told me for the millionth time never to look at a glass as half empty.

The HIV test result I collected from the renowned hospital at Klongkak a long time ago was right under my bed amidst piles of papers and books. Demas kept encouraging me to find it. But he didn't know that it was hidden in the queerest of all places. That was a piece of paper both Demas and I had never bothered to look very closely at. I did not know how to convince Demas to step outside so that I pull it out of my outdated trunk and give it one more look before he came back. An idea came to mind that I should tell him that I was thirsty and needed a soft drink. I made the proposal before realizing that we had bought some drinks at the bakery when we left Dr. Che Richard's clinic. Typical of Demas, he merely took one of the cold bottles of the fruit drink, opened it, drank a bit, and gave me the bottle.

I took the drink and sat comfortably in bed and began sipping it. He was so anxious to view the results because he kept moving his body parts uncontrollably. When he saw that I was wasting time, he said that I was not serious about it being under my bed. He brought down my box from my closet and placed it before me to open. When I repeated that it was under my bed, he still did not believe me. It was only when I bent down to pull out the trunk from under the bed that he held me up and told me that he would do it. I knew it wasn't going to be easy getting to the trunk because it was junky beneath my bed. Besides, there was also some food under my bed as well, which made me feel ashamed.

Demas wasted no time in pulling off his tie and folding his trousers up to his knee to begin the ordeal of bringing out the old trunk. He also pulled off his oxblood shirt and was only left with his white inner wear. Afterwards, he crawled on his belly under the bed. There, he asked me which box it was because he found a lot of stuff. I told him to first remove the things because the trunk was right behind. After battling for close to ten minutes, he crawled out with the trunk; drenched in his own sweat. The old trunk was smeared with patches of rust and cobwebs. I was tapping my leg uneasily. We could hear rattling noises emanating from the trunk

When I opened the box, two rats and a host of cockroaches crawled out of the trunk. Demas tried killing the rats with one of his shoes but his efforts were in vain as both rats scampered up the wall and vamoosed through the ceiling. When Demas came back from his fruitless attempt to kill the rats, I was more confused and ashamed because the trunk contained a pile of shredded papers as if they had been chopped by an outdated blender. I rummaged through the soft pieces of papers to look for the file containing the test result. When I pulled out the half-destroyed grey file, a pungent smell emanated from the trunk. Demas closed his nostrils with his fingers as three or so baby rats started squeaking and struggling to come out of the trunk. Miraculously, the paper containing the test results were intact. All other papers like my transcripts were completely pulverized by the insects and rodents.

With trembling hands, I opened the folded paper but to our utter dismay part of the area where my name was written had been eaten by the rodents and insects. I gave the paper to Demas who scrutinized it carefully and drew my attention to something which made me believe I was dreaming in broad daylight. At first, I waved it aside. It was only when he pointed at it again that I took time to really look at it. The last name was missing, but the last three letters of my first name on the paper were LYA! I plodded over to the window, brought the paper closer to my eyes and confirmed the three strange letters.

But how SHA could become LYA was the puzzle we had to unravel. My heartbeat was increasing at an alarming rate. I turned around to see Demas saying repeatedly in firmly closed eyes

"Thank you, God…"

When he opened his eyes he said, "I knew it… I told you…"

"I am dumbfounded."

Still pacing up and down, he muttered, "I believe in miracles."

"So, what do we do now?"

"We're going to Klongkak now." Before he could finish his speech, his shirt was already on and he was putting on his tie at the threshold of the door.

While on the way he put his hand on his head as if seriously trying to recall something. When I asked what it was, he merely waved off my question saying, "Wait…wait…wait…" while still scratching his head. Then he said "Oohh I can now remember—

"What?"

"The day we did the test the counselor asked me to assist him in arranging some envelopes in the cabinet messed up by the se—"

"What about that?"

"I saw a name that looked like yours."

"It was surely not mine." I hurriedly stopped him from raising my hopes only for them to be dashed again.

Along the ride to Klongkak, I saw so many soldiers who lined the streets as if there was going to be a coup. I grew more nervous. I was so tensed until someone in the taxi said that the president would likely be leaving the country because major roads in the city had been blocked since 6 a.m. When we reached Provence, the situation was worse. The way to Klongkak was not as smooth as we'd thought as it became clear that the president's motorcade was leaving for the airport. After waiting for about half an hour, the taxi driver finally dropped us on the way and took a different route. He regretted that his whole day would be messed up since we were his first clients. He complained that he had a pregnant wife and sick child, and the cost of living was too high.

But guess what? It was not even the president who had occupied the presidential bullet-proof limousine. Conspicuously seated in the backseat of the most expensive car in both West and Central Africa were the president's wife and his daughter. News filtered amongst passersby that the head of state's wife was escorting her daughter to the US to enroll her at the University of Harvard. We wasted about three hours waiting because even after the president's convoy had left, the roads were still blocked.

At Klongkak the same counselor who had advised us before and after the HIV test was even more confused. He went to the logbook where test results of patients were written. After going through it, he stopped and started shaking his head and blinking his eyes.

"Anything the matter?" Demas asked.

He stood like a pillar. His lips twitching. His nose fraying.

I stood up. "Have you seen anything sir?"

He took a deep breath and said, "I don't know how to put it."

Demas said, "We're children of God and are able to brave the storms of life."

The counselor began trembling, picking his nose and blinking his eyes. His mouth curved into a smile. He fidgeted a little, yawned, supported his head with his hands and drawled, "We are...no I am truly sorry for the trouble you've gone through."

"We still don't get you," Demas said widening his eyes.

"I think there was a big mistake somewhere."

My heart fluttered.

"Where? How?" We both asked at once.

He stood up, sat down again, opened drawers and closed them before telling us to calm down. He said the blunder was made by the secretary who took Natasha for Natalya. He said the secretary had long been fired by the new no-nonsense director of the hospital. He said he was sorry for the mix up and said the situation had remained that way because Natalya never came back for her results. He added that his poor eyesight had confounded the problem.

The world narrowed to a dot. When I regained consciousness, I could not still believe my eyes. Tears of joy trickled down my cheeks in rivulets as I continually brushed my palms together. I muttered several times to myself, "Thank God I did not tell my parents that I was HIV positive." When I lifted my head to see what Demas was doing, I saw him exhibiting what looked like early signs of dementia. He threw his hands in the air several times. He stood. He sat. He covered his eyes with his hands. I then skipped over two chairs and embraced Demas passionately, who was jumping at one corner with his hands raised. He burst into speaking in tongues— that heavenly esoteric language born again Christians use in certain circumstances. The counselor was amazed and dumbfounded by this strange language. Tears of joy were streaming down my cheeks. Then I sang a popular chorus:

There's no one, there's no one like Jesus...
I turn round; turn round, no on...no one...
I search, search, search, search, no one...no one...

The counselor joined us, and we danced like King David.

Afterwards, he told us to kneel down so he could lay his hands on our heads and pray. When we stood up after the Holy Spirit-filled prayer, I peered into Demas's sparking eyes and burst into song and dance. The counselor began wiggling his shoulders before twisting his torso as if it were boneless. When the excitement in us swallowed him, he cast caution aside and gamboled like a gazelle. The commotion brought some nurses around. We paid no attention to them and danced until we were doused in sweat.

I embraced Demas passionately planting a wet kiss on his lips. As we swaggered out of the hospital, I was telling everyone that I was H-I-V negative. I also told myself that I would tell Dr. Neba of Affordable Health Clinic that I was a free person who had been living in chains out of ignorance. I vividly remembered Mark Twain's famous words: "Some of the worst things in my life never happened."

At the entrance to the hospital, Demas nestled into me, peered into my eyes, smiled and said, "Natasha, my love…what God has put together…"

I chortled, shook my hips, and replied, "let no man put asunder!"

About the Author

Timothy Keyeke Mbombo holds a BA in English and a master's degree in American Literature from the University of Yaoundé I. He also graduated with a diploma in education from the Higher Teachers' Training College, Yaoundé. He obtained a diploma in creative writing from Stratford Career Institute and a master's in English and Creative Writing from Southern New Hampshire University. Mbombo also holds a BSc in Journalism and Mass Communication from the University of Ashford and teaches in the Washington County in the USA.

About Spears Books

Spears Books is an independent publisher dedicated to providing innovative publication strategies with emphasis on African/Africana stories and perspectives. As a platform for alternative voices, we prioritize the accessibility and affordability of our titles in order to ensure that relevant and often marginal voices are represented at the global marketplace of ideas. Our titles – poetry, fiction, narrative nonfiction, memoirs, reference, travel writing, African languages, and young people's literature – aim to bring African worldviews closer to diverse readers. Our titles are distributed in paperback and electronic formats globally by African Books Collective.

Visit us at www.spearsmedia.com

CONNECT WITH US

Visit our Website

Go to www.spearsmedia.com to learn about exclusive previews and read excerpts of new books, find detailed information on our titles, authors, subject area books, and special discounts.

Subscribe to our Free Newsletter

Be amongst the first to hear about our newest publications, special discount offers, news about bestsellers, author interviews, coupons and more! Subscribe to our newsletter by visiting www.spearsmedia. com

Quantity Discounts

Spears Books are available at quantity discounts for orders of ten or more copies. Contact African Books Collectives at orders@african-bookscollective.com or Spears Books at orders@spearsmedia.com.

Host a Reading Group

Learn more about how to host a reading group on our website at www.spearsmedia.comv

Printed in the United States
By Bookmasters